SEARCHING
for the
REMARKABLE
in THINGS

SEARCHING *for the* REMARKABLE *in* THINGS

NATALIE LUCY

First published in the UK in 2025 by ZunTold
www.zuntold.com

Text copyright © Natalie Lucy 2025
Cover design by Isla Bousfield-Donohoe

The moral right of the author has been asserted.
All rights reserved.
Unauthorised duplication contravenes existing laws.

A catalogue record for this book is available
from the British Library

ISBN: 978-1-915758-132
10 8 6 4 2 1 3 5 7 9

Printed and bound by Interak, Poland

*To my parents, who shaped my world.
My mum, who always believed in the existence of magic,
and my dad who tried to teach us to never judge
and who was always decent and kind.*

Prologue

Clover

I don't remember everything. Bits come back to me in tiny flashes. The colour of his eyes, blue-green like the sea. The smell of soap and coffee, clinging to his jumper, which felt soft as it brushed my face. Or the warmth of his massive hands, fingers bent over each of mine. Strong. And safe.

Until he left.

I must have got used to it at some point, Dad being gone, and it being just us. Probably because Mum created a kind of magic, all spun together in a sparkling web which wrapped around me and made me feel special. And because she told me that I could do remarkable things if I wanted to enough, her indigo eyes shimmering so much they reminded me of jewels.

I didn't have as big an imagination, though. I couldn't paint a sky like she did with little fragments of light that looked like perfect, sparkling stars, and vivid splashes of colour in violet and purple. Sometimes things got stuck in my brain. But I still believed her. I still thought that if I wanted to do something so much that it lodged itself inside my head, then I could. I believed her right up until the day she died, when I searched for the secret box, I knew she kept hidden, because I wanted to find a bit of her to cling on to, so that the pain wouldn't take over and make me feel like I was drowning.

I didn't find any pieces of magic in it, though. I just found lies.

But among all the things in the box that didn't make sense, was a small piece of cloth, wrapped in layers of tissue paper and patterned with shapes that reminded me of birds. And a stack of letters, old and creased into a thousand lines and tied together with a purple ribbon.

The letter at the top was written in 1851, over one hundred and seventy years ago, and thousands of miles away, in Georgia, USA. I nearly left it because I didn't get how it could possibly have anything to do with Mum or me but, as soon as I started reading the words, something made me jolt. It was as if I could hear the voice of the girl out loud, her words urgent, as if they were pounded out to the rhythm of a drum.

I had always sensed her somehow. Someone else, breathing beside me. Not a sister exactly. More like a friend. It had been my secret, especially just after Dad had left, or when Mum was ill, and I'd lain lonely and scared in my bed at night, eyes closed tight even though I hated the dark. And even though the letters seemed to be telling a different story from the one I'd imagined when I tried to get to sleep, I still felt like I'd heard the voices before, carried from some distant place, like a whisper of the breeze across the sea.

And so, I knew.

That the letters were not just about Mary, or even Mum. They were also somehow about *me* . . .

January, 1851
Dear R,

I'm Mary. No middle or end to it – just Mary.

My momma always told me that, one day, remarkable things would happen to me. 'No, Mary,' I hear her say, voice dripping like treacle, 'not happen *to you – you will* do *remarkable things.'*

Not right now though, with no room to properly breathe – and nowhere to look but the sky above or the earth pressed flat under my feet, working from dawn till the sun sets low and cerise and crimson form bands across the sky. For now, my space to breathe is inside. Deep, deep within my chest – or heart – so that nobody can touch it.

Because that's where I write my story. Not what other people do or say, but my proper story – the bit I cling to so tight that sometimes I don't even hear anyone ask me anything or call out my name. Because that's when part of me can whoosh straight up into the sky and float on those soft clouds like an ocean in the air. And then I can forget I'm out in the fields, picking cotton until my hands are rubbed raw, my eyes squinting so much I can barely see for all the little blotches when I blink.

Reuben can't do that, though. And not because he's only seven and I'm near fifteen. It's because he can't work out how to grow his story inside him. 'Reuben,' I say, 'it's like Momma told us – you have to feed it. And if anything at all threatens it, you gotta cover it right on over, creating a hard shell.'

But, standing on the porch at the new place, my hair brushed so hard it feels like little grooves running all over my scalp, I don't think I can keep that story part intact, even though I grit down on my teeth with my chin up high so nobody can try to put me down.

'Please, Mary, you can't go as well,' Reuben whispers,

~ 3 ~

because Momma's been gone three years now, since that day the speculators came and chained up all the people they thought they'd get good money for. They took her and Pete, who's a bit like a daddy to me, and led them off like animals.

'Never forget,' Momma said, eyes fierce, although she didn't really seem like Momma, because even when her shell was up around her – and to anyone else seemed like wood and rock – she could still turn to me and flash that wide smile from one side of her head to the other. As if she just went right on up and snatched down a few stars from the sky to make her eyes sparkle.

So here I am. Trying to keep on growing my story inside, my fists tightly clenched, as I stare straight ahead at the big wide door. It opens bit by bit until I see a girl of about my age. She looks like a china doll, all yellow curls and a lilac dress with frills of lace in waves.

I won't be here long, *I want my eyes to say, but then I breathe. And then I breathe again and something inside me turns that sick feeling deep within my stomach into the pitter-patter of a little story bird. Until I almost feel like me.*

Chapter One

Clover

January

'Clover, time to go,' Dad calls up the stairs. It's 8.30 a.m. and he's doing that fake-cheery voice again. He speaks like that when he doesn't want to show that he's annoyed or sad, which he does quite a lot. I brush my hair for the twentieth time, hoping it will look 'brunette' or even 'chestnut' in the right light and not just drab and mid-brown. But it's still the same dull reflection in the mirror – grey-blue eyes and a smattering of freckles on what Mum called a 'heart-shaped face'– nothing *wrong* exactly, but just, well, *ordinary*.

I pick up my bag, grabbing a book from the bedside cabinet – *Noughts and Crosses* by Malorie Blackman, bought last week to add to the shelf, which was already full of books. There was a whole mix of things that Dad put there in the first few days after I arrived – Louis Sacher and Katherine Rundell, but also the Brontës and George Eliot. So, even if he hadn't made any effort to contact me since I was six years old, I suppose he tried to think about me. Unless he didn't . . .and it was Caroline, the social worker they sent the day Mum died, who told him I liked books. Her or the psychologist who sat with me for two hours, trying to be kind and telling me that everything I felt was 'quite normal', except that I saw the quick scribbling of notes and could guess what they thought. *Difficulties socially. Resentment towards father. Lonely.*

'Well, don't you look great?' Dad says as I come down the stairs.

'Well, in a boring kind of way . . .' I say, glancing down at my black jersey skirt and maroon top. My face scrunches up. I don't mean to, but I can't stop myself doing it.

'What do you mean?' Dad asks. 'Do you mean the clothes? I think they're suitable for a first day of school – fairly neutral.'

'Yes, they're definitely neutral,' I say, wishing I could learn to keep my mouth shut. Especially when I notice the wave of sadness settling on his face.

'You look good,' Dad says, jangling the car keys. 'Are you ready to go?'

'Yep,' I say, wanting to make the noise stop.

The car windows are streaked with rain, but I stare out, trying to stop myself from fiddling with my fingers because the psychologist frowned when I did that and scribbled down more words. I try to grip them together, pressing my index and middle fingers to my thumbs, and fix my eyes on the rows of identical redbrick houses with square patches of grass at the front. This time, I try to convince myself, school will feel better and, if I don't act like some kind of freak, I might even manage to make a friend. But that makes me feel sick again, because I don't even know what girls my age talk about, except they probably don't obsess about the way leaves get water from the soil. Or spend hours trying to work out the perfect paint for the green of a plant's stem or the mix of browns and greys you need for the bark of a tree. So, I have to try to talk about something normal. Not just art stuff that most people would think was weird.

I practise smiling in the wing mirror, moving my mouth around to see what looks best, but it still feels like there's a dead rock buried deep down somewhere in my chest, and I catch myself with a slightly freaky frozen expression on my face. But then Dad laughs – not a cackle or that big, enormous laugh that Mum would have done – but a little light bubble, mouth closed and eyes shining. 'That's better,' he says.

The school's ugly – yellow bricks and glass, apart from the neatly mown grass all around it in lush lime green, and what look like tree stumps. Ms Beech, the head teacher, tells me it's a 'trim trail'. I can tell from the little sympathetic smile she shoots me before she and Dad disappear into her office that she knows I don't know what that is. They're in there for ages, so I stare at the clock on the wall, only half aware of the jerking of the hands until, eventually, the door swings open and Ms Beech marches out, Dad trailing behind.

'So, Clover, what are your favourite subjects?' Ms Beech asks. She isn't what I'd expected – she has long limbs and shiny dark hair cut perfectly into a straight bob. Like one of those pictures on the hair dye boxes Mum used when she said she felt like 'going red' for a few weeks, although Mum's hair always looked like she'd stepped out of a salon anyway. Sleek and beautiful.

'Clover,' Ms Beech asks me – that same voice, rich like silky black coffee. 'What subjects do you like?'

'Art,' I eventually stutter out, 'and history.' I try to

force my voice to lift a little. I don't want her to think I'm a complete idiot.

'Clover's schooling has been unconventional so far,' Dad says. 'She reads a lot, though,' he adds.

That's true: *Jane Eyre* and *1984* and *The Great Gatsby* because they were on Mum's bookshelves. All the classics that were supposed to be 'too old' for me, but I still understood them, looking up the difficult words until it all made sense. Mum wanted to discuss the themes and some of the symbolism. 'There's significance in the names too,' I remember offering. 'Rivers and Reeds and Eyre – like *air*.'

'Of course,' she said, smiling, briefly surprised. 'How did I not notice that?'

So, it's not comprehension that stops me answering simple questions people ask me. It's something else that stops my mouth moving.

'Well, shall we go in?' Ms Beech suggests. 'The class is making jewellery. It's part of a topic on the Aztecs.'

I open my mouth to say *yes*, but something funny happens in my chest and my heart's beating too quickly and too *hard*.

'Clover?' Dad asks softly. 'Do you want to go in?'

I can see through the window that all the tables are crammed in together, everyone leaning over and into each other, brushing arms or legs or hands without seeming to notice.

'I suppose so,' I say, even though my heart's still beating too fast.

When I walk into the room, everyone stops still, although Ms Gupta the class teacher, smiles at me and points to a space next to a girl called Heather who has auburn hair in low bunchies.

'Hello,' Heather says, smiling. 'Do you want me to show

you how to do this?' She holds up a piece of wire and some sort of metal tool. 'Your name is cool,' she goes on, when I don't reply. 'I wish I had a more exciting name. For some reason, my parents decided to call my sister Seraphina and then called me a boring old name like Heather . . .'

'But it's nice,' I stutter. It's actually a bit like *my* name, natural and a little bit wild. Our names even sound the same, but my smile feels weird again, like it's set like stone. 'It's really pretty,' I mumble. 'It's . . .'

I don't finish my sentence, and Heather looks at me with a small smile on her face, trying to be patient as she waits for me to carry on but, even though it should be the easiest thing in the world, I can't.

'This is how you do it,' Heather says eventually, gathering up a piece of wire. 'You have to put those beads on a section of wire and then twist it . . .' She plays around with the wire, using the tool to bend it into different shapes, like hearts and stars. She laughs – a little giggle and then reaches over to the beads and wire in front of me. 'Like this.' But then she accidentally touches my hand, and I flinch, and her smile evaporates. 'Sorry,' she says.

I want to try to explain that I'm just not used to school. Or people. Because I like Heather, and the way her smile is like a flash across her face, white teeth showing, and eyes crinkling in the corners. But I suddenly sense myself flushing, bright and hot, and have to look down. I try to focus on the table and the wire and the beads, but it's too late, because my fingers and arms are trembling and, even though Heather's looking at me, I can't answer.

It's like she's *outside* something whereas I'm *inside* – but trapped, like there's a wall around me, concrete and hard. Everything outside is muffled and blurred and all I can hear is Mum's voice, her laugh tinkling like a bell, her eyes glowing. For a moment, I'm there again, standing by the grave – rocking, rocking, trying not to fall over or fall in – as I hear the heavy soil being chucked onto the wood. I want to cry out: *Mum wouldn't want to be in a box. She hated being shut in.* She always wanted the bristling breeze on her face, floating through the open stable backdoor as she mixed the paint, a smear of claret red on her left cheek, as she smiled. An exotic tropical bird – tall and slim with flashes of colour.

'Are you alright?' Heather asks quietly.

I nod, although it's just a little tremor. If I could just find something solid, something I could focus on, maybe I could stop my heart from doing that loud pounding drumming.

I look out of the window and see a red-breasted robin – a splash of colour on the bare branches of a tree – as it flits to the bird feeder, pecking away at the meshing. My heart slows down and I don't think I'm going to faint at least, but I still feel like I'm somewhere else until I hear the distant echo of Ms Gupta's kind voice saying, '*Clover? Clover?*' and the nervous giggles of children.

Chapter Two

Clover

I'm sitting outside Ms Beech's office again. It's two weeks after that first day. I thought school would get easier, but it hasn't. I still feel hemmed in and panicked every time I'm in the classroom. And I still hate the noise of the canteen, even if it's supposed to be a 'bohemian' school or however Dad described it.

I stare at the clock, trying to shut out the hum of voices. They left the door open for me in case I wanted to join them, but I can tell they don't want me to hear. Dad's gravelly voice is low, although I can tune into it if I focus enough.

'I knew school would be a challenge, but I hoped that, as this is a small school with a more relaxed ethos, it might have been less daunting,' he says. 'Clover's thirteen, but she hasn't been to school at all. What with leaving her home in Scotland and her mother's death it's been really difficult for her . . .' For a few seconds there's silence but then he goes on. 'I don't really know her. So I don't know how to help her.' I listen to the clock ticking. 'When I first brought her to live with me, Clover said she wanted to carry on being homeschooled, but I don't think I'm capable of that – maths and economics maybe, but I have to work, and I'd be hopeless at the arts. And anyway, things will get harder from now on, I mean, if she was in school she'd need to think about options and then GCSEs and she's really behind...' I study my fingers, wiggling them around. His voice is just a whisper, but I can still hear the tremble. 'Deciding to come to school wasn't as much about exam results though . . . I think she was lonely.'

I sit up, my face burning. How can Dad worry about whether I was lonely or how I did at schoolwork when he's not even been around until now? All those years, from when I was six until now, it's been me and Mum. And we did OK without him. Because we were a team and had an amazing connection or whatever Mum used to call it. But then I remember Mum's secret box. And I'm not sure about anything.

I can just make out Ms Beech's reply: 'Maybe we should just continue for a bit longer. It's early days.' There's a pause. 'Although Clover seems very withdrawn.'

I hear someone sigh, which I think must be Dad, and then Ms Beech's crisp voice again. 'What do the doctors say?'

I switch off after that, watching the clock on the wall until even that and its endless ticking makes me think of Mum and the small house in Scotland with the big clock in the hallway. Most of the time it was just background noise but sometimes, when Mum was upstairs asleep, and I was painting or reading a book by myself in the kitchen it was the only thing I could hear.

After a few minutes Ms Beech opens the door. 'Do you want to come in?' she suggests smiling.

I go in, sitting down in the chair next to Dad. His left leg is trembling.

'We wondered if it would be a good idea to take some

time out,' he says. 'Maybe a few months away. You could keep up with your schoolwork online, but we'd have lots of time to relax and explore . . .A sort of road trip,' he says.

Heather brings my bag out to the hallway at break time. Dad is still talking to Ms Beech. They are talking about worksheets and how to catch up on all those subjects I'm pretty useless at like science and maths. 'I put all your things in there,' Heather says, her eyes opening wide as she studies me. 'That jewellery we made on your first day is at the top, so it doesn't get all bent out of shape.' She hands the bag to me. 'I thought you'd want to keep all your art as well. It's *really* good.'

'Thank you,' I say, flushing bright red. 'Thank you for being so nice to me.' The words catch in my throat. 'I mean, this isn't because of you or anyone else. It's just . . .' I swallow. 'I'm not used to school.' I can't tell her everything, though. She'll think it's weird and that something must be *really* wrong with me. 'It's just, school makes me feel kind of hemmed in.'

'It's OK,' Heather says, handing me a piece of paper. 'This is my phone number and address. I mean, if you want to, you know, Snapchat or write or something.'

'Thank you,' I say.

'Maybe you'll come back to this school later on,' she says.

I try to make my mouth turn up, I want to smile at least because she's being so nice.

I don't know if she can tell, but Heather suddenly flashes a big wide smile so that her eyes dance around and I almost want to stay.

Chapter Three

Mary

January 1851
Dear R,

Reuben couldn't come to the new place. They only wanted a girl. And I'm apparently the 'right age' at fifteen. Standing on the front porch that day, the sun and breeze full in my face, it feels like a rock hurtling at me even though I try not to think about Reuben too much. Hannah said that these people were liberal folk, whatever that means. 'Child,' she said to me, gripping my shoulder a little too tightly so that I can feel that pressure even now, 'they're much better than this Massa Bolt here . . . and anyhow, you'll be out of that terrible sun, eating all the pickings those grand folk leave over and not breaking your back in the cotton fields no more.'

'What about Reuben?' I asked, because he'd still have to get up at five in the morning and drag himself out to the yard at the bell, even though the sun soon beat down so hard it made your head pound.

'I'll look after Reuben good,' Hannah said, squeezing him tight. I knew she would. I remember the marks on her from when she was tied to a tree out under the bright sun. Whipped until her back looked like a hand of twigs on a *branch in winter just for helping Momma when she was forced out into the fields, even though the baby was about to drop out of her, and nearly did, except that he was breach, and it was too long and painful for him to make it into this world.*

But Reuben just stared at me. 'Now, you make sure you look down, Reuben,' I pleaded, knowing Momma wouldn't want us to look down about anything. 'Don't you ever let them catch your eye.'

I am still thinking about Reuben and Hannah when the porch door opens. It makes me jolt but I shake my head making myself focus my eyes on her.

'I'm Ruby,' the girl says. She's about my age. Fourteen or fifteen, anyhow. She doesn't smile. Just studies me like I'm vaguely interesting before she marches along, her feet bouncing like she's dancing. I follow her, neither of us saying a thing, until she opens a door to a kitchen. She looks at me, her eyes running over my hair that Hannah washed and brushed so hard it shone, even though I was gritting my teeth, both hands flat on my head so that she couldn't pull it out at the roots. 'People are always telling me that fair is better,' Ruby says, studying her own golden curls with a little upturned lip, 'but your hair is real nice.' She smiles. 'You should wait in here. Tildy will be back in a minute. She'll tell you everything.' She smiles again, which is a tiny crinkle of her eyes and a dazzle of something white before she gives a little toss of her head and goes away.

I look around at the kitchen. It's all shiny with scrubbed floors and there are rows and rows of pans dangling from the ceiling by lines of string which look like spiders' legs. It's quiet and the air is filled with the smell of herbs and bread just out of the oven and, for a flickering of a second, I'm almost pleased. But then I remember Reuben's thin arms and his jutting-out jaw. And his gradual wide smile that creeps across his face when he shows me the things he found in his 'special place' – under the rock by the back of the cabin, where bugs and worms and beetles squirm and run around.

'You the girl from the Bolt place?' I nearly jump. It's a woman of about forty or fifty. Her voice sounds stern but when she studies me her eyes are round and bright. 'What's your name?' she asks.

'Mary,' I say.

'How old are you? They told us a girl coming but Massa Finch promise his sister that he not gonna buy real, living people like they just his things anymore.'

'I'm near fifteen,' I say.

'Mighty scrawny,' she says. 'They treat you bad at that Bolt place?'

I nod, biting my lip.

She touches my arm and it's like a shot of warmth. 'You leave any of your folks there?'

'My brother,' I say.

She tuts and shakes her head. 'The evil these people do,' she mutters.

'This all we have to do?' I ask Tildy when she shows me round *the kitchen later.*

'You wash up, you clean up and you do whatever you told to do, child,' Tildy says. 'Without complaining about it . . .' I don't know why but her eyes seem to twinkle when she speaks, and I like her already.

'That's not too bad,' I say, without thinking. 'Compared to picking cotton, I mean.'

Tildy looks stern for a second. 'It might be better here, but don't you make the mistake of thinking this is easy. I do my job well, but I don't do my job too well, if you know what I mean, which keeps me just about alright in my head and heart.' Tildy grips her right fist tight. *'But still not free.'* She scowls at me. *'And even if the Finch folks are better than some, still plenty of folk on this plantation don't see things the way the Finches do.'*

'Tildy.' I almost jump at the sound of a voice at the doorway. It's a boy, about sixteen or seventeen years old, with big grey-green eyes and dark hair in thick kinks which fly off in a whole heap of different directions. *'Tildy, have you seen my books anywhere?'* he asks. I think Tildy might get angry except he's not issuing orders like Massa Bolt's evil son used to all the time. I used to run past him to make certain I wouldn't catch his eye.

'Yes, I did. Back in your room, Master Benjamin. Make a change you try looking there.'

Massa Bolt would have whipped you raw for that, but Benjamin just smiles. 'Oh, thank you,' he says, fixing his eyes on me, which are like pebbles shining at the bottom of a deep pool. *'Who are you?'* he asks shyly.

'I'm Mary.' My voice trails away. He won't stop staring. And not like most white folks look at me, their chins high in the air, but like he actually sees something.

'Master Benjamin!' Tildy says, chuckling until redness tinges his whole face, and he mutters, *'Sorry,'* before trudging on off.

'I reckon he's taken a shine to you, Mary girl,' Tildy says, with another low laugh, which sounds like rasping and wheezing all mixed in together. *'He's a good boy . . . at the moment.'* She shakes her head, apparently lost in thought, as she opens a sack of flour, creating small clouds as she claps them tight together, leaving a thin layer of white on her hands. *'Just hope he don't get his head turned around and all mixed*

up once he grows up,' she adds. *'Plenty of good souls been twisted about by the world out there.'*

That first day passes quick. We work hard and Tildy seems kind. She doesn't holler at least when I get things wrong, she just shows me in a calm way how to do the cooking and cleaning. I don't see Ruby again. And I don't even see Massa Finch, although Tildy says that most times he leave us alone.

In the evening, after we eventually finish all the work, my arms and legs and brain aching so much I want to collapse, we sit together outside the cabin. I can see the house in the distance, but it still feels like our own special circle, where the spirits can live, and we are protected from the world. The oldest woman, Harriet, sits in the middle, her shoulders heaving and hands outstretched as she tells us a story against the breeze on the night air while crickets chirp in the distance. I look around at the circle. Everyone's eyes are wide, like Harriet is spinning some kind of special magic as she tells a story about Brer Rabbit tricking Brer Fox until everyone laughs and, for a few moments, it feels like we are free.

It's late when we go to bed. It's the first time I can properly think about Reuben. I wish he was here with me. Least people don't get beaten half the time and there are extra bits of food. *'You would not believe what they think is good enough to waste,'* Tildy muttered to me earlier that day, quickly handing me a piece of cornbread. *'Would keep our whole cabin full up for a month.'*

The cabin is pretty much the same, though. It's made of wood with a dirt floor although there are some rough rugs on the ground. There are five of us in the cabin. At the Bolts there were twelve, although Tildy says that the cabins for those who

~ 18 ~

work in the fields all day long are worse than this one and it's still cramped and dark.

I sleep next to Tildy and Martha on one side. Libby and Rachel are on the other side of the room, so close I feel Rachel's foot touch mine a few times in the night. Libby is quite old. Maybe fifty. She tell me she was here when Thomas Finch owned the plantation. Supposed to be Iris's servant, but Massa Finch's sister grew up and went to the north and never came back. Rachel is about twenty-five. She don't like me much. Just nods her head at me occasionally. Martha is Tildy's daughter. About twenty and a hand's span taller than me with wiry, strong arms. She has a sharp tongue you don't want to get the end of, but she loves her momma, puts her arms around her all the time, leaning her head on her shoulder as we sat around listening to stories and music after supper, like they are two parts of one person.

I hate the darkness, so when Martha is breathing deep next to me, I try to listen for the owls and their strange haunting sound like song, as I search around for some light. Just when my heart is racing so much, I think it might burst on out of my chest, I find a small glimmer of the moon seeping in through the cracks of the wooden slats and can breathe a little.

And then I turn inside out and picture myself as that bird, lit brightly by the moon and able to fly free. And imagine Reuben next to me, telling him just as if he were the one lying beside me: 'In my story inside, we're going on a big adventure. And you're not in those fields now with the sun burning on out. Instead, we're walking on right out of the plantation, for miles, pausing in the woods, our feet crunching dry twigs and the birds calling to each other all around, surrounding us with this magical circle of sound.

'And then we find a stream, and you can just sit there, searching under the rocks for bugs, while dragonflies flap their

wings as they hover above, adding a dash of silver-blue to the picture.

'And I just take my shoes off and I wade on into that lovely water.

'With the air on my face.'

Chapter Four

Clover

March

'Clover.' It's Dad. Rapping twice at the door of my bedroom at the youth hostel. We've been here for a few weeks now. We didn't expect to stay anywhere. Dad said a 'field trip' would help us to 'get to know each other' and that it might be easier for me to 'heal' without any pressures. But then we got to Cornwall and saw the turquoise sea and the enormous sky, and we both wanted to stay.

'Coming,' I call, as breezily as I can manage. I put the letters back in the box, and I wrap the tissue carefully around the piece of fabric that I found there too. It's about the length and width of my hand and has a pale pink background. For some reason, the strange black triangles always make me think of birds flying – although, when I look again, they're just geometrical shapes. Just *lines*, which don't seem to mean much.

So maybe it isn't special . . . Except for the fact that it was in the *secret* box. 'This is my only rule. Nothing else. Just this one tiny corner of privacy,' Mum always told me, which I hated, because it was supposed to just be me and her. That's what she said, anyway. And some days, when we'd make cookies together and she'd say we could be as messy as we liked and sit in front of the fire with real chocolate melting into mugs of steaming milk, playing Scrabble or sketching out funny little cartoons of people and animals, it was nearly perfect. Sometimes I think I might have invented it all, but then I remember Mum's eyes flickering with the reflection of the flames and know it was real.

I gently place the fabric back into the box, beneath the photographs and letters. The box was the only thing I took from the house. Well, that and the painting, which is still resting against the wall at Dad's house.

Dad never asked why I changed my mind, darting back at the last moment into the little house in Scotland, as we were about to drive away from everything I had ever known. But it was the only one of Mum's paintings I wanted to keep. All the others made me all churned up inside – because the days after she finished them were usually difficult. Mum would lay flat on her back on her bed all morning, eyes closed, as she listened to Prokofiev or Mahler.

I never told the social workers – the 'do-gooders', as Mum called them – but homeschooling wasn't *always* about quizzes on Greek culture or talking about Emily Brontë's poetry. There were a lot of days when I'd just wander around the garden, searching for leaves or flowers, pulling them apart, petal by petal, before I'd paint them in the kitchen. I can still remember the faint smell of dust and paint as I struggled to mix up the exact colour for a leaf – bright luminous green or a deep red – because it had to be right. It had to be *accurate*.

'It doesn't matter. It can be anything you want it to

be. You can have an indigo sky and an emerald sea below,' Mum sometimes said, but I hated it when she said that, because I knew what all the comments about being creative meant: she thought I had no imagination.

So, the only picture I wanted was Mum's last one. Painted in one night, the doors closed tight as she threw splashes of purple and orange onto a canvas which, by morning, looked magical. And three weeks later, on a Thursday morning when the rain pounded down on the windows again, she stopped breathing, and it felt like the world was going to end. So maybe my heart wasn't any more powerful than my imagination.

The day after she died, I tiptoed into her workshop to look at the painting. It was still there on its easel: a valley in lush greens as a turquoise river meandered through it, birds in the indigo sky above it. I don't know how long I stared at it before the social worker Caroline appeared beside me, pausing her search for details about Dad, because I was supposed to be packing an overnight bag.

'Sorry,' I said.

'It's beautiful,' she said.

But that wasn't why I stared at it. I was trying to fix an image of Mum somewhere inside the picture so that I could get rid of the horrible one lodged in my brain: Mum surrounded by tubes and machines in the hospital with the green walls and the smell of chemicals. But in the painting, Mum could forever be suspended in a world of colour. Not with angels or anything like that, but in her type of heaven.

'*Clover!*' It's Dad again, knocking at the door. 'Come on. We agreed. School work in the mornings and free time in the afternoons.' He sighs. 'Look Clover, I get that it's hard. It's just you've had four weeks off school already.'

I put the box into the wardrobe, trying not to make too much noise.

'Alright in there?' Dad calls when I drop the box, and it makes a loud thudding sound.

'Yep,' I say, throwing the pile of jumpers and tops over the box.

I yank on a jumper and jeans from a little heap on the floor, flinging open the door and nudging past Dad, surprised at the sensation of wool and the warm rush up my arm. Ms Delauney is downstairs in the dining room, sitting in the window, writing. Dad said she's 'an academic' and she's always there when I come down for breakfast, sometimes sitting so still that she seems like a statue, her face frozen in the window as she holds her pen, deep in thought.

I grab a bowl of cornflakes from the kitchen, spilling a little milk over the sides as I walk back to the dining room.

'Oh, Clover,' Ms Delauney calls out, her eyes flicking around the room. 'I wondered if you'd join me for a walk later . . . a sort of field trip.'

'What kind of field trip?' I glance at Dad, wondering if he'd asked her to take me, because he and the psychologist think I'm such a 'loner', but he's eating his toast, a newspaper open beside my schoolbooks and, when I look back at Ms Delauney, her face just seems open.

'I'm researching for my new book. It's all about the myths and legends that abound in Cornwall, and I thought you might be able to help.'

I nod. Ms Delauney seems nice now that I have got used to the way she sometimes speaks like she's in one of those black and white 1950s film's Mum liked. And at least I won't have to spend hours with Dad trying to make conversation, or him suggesting games of Scrabble or cards, although it's now less awkward than those first few weeks when we drove through Dorset and Devon, permanently playing music or listening to radio programmes in the car so we wouldn't have to speak.

'Shall we go after lunch? I'm sure your dad won't mind if you do all those dry worksheets later.' I glance over at Dad. He nods and then tilts his head with a little half smile. I know he wants me to say something.

'OK,' I say in the end. 'Thank you,' I add when I remember.

'So, Clover, how are you enjoying your trip?' Ms Delauney asks later, as we trudge across the heath, the sun already weak in the sky.

'It's been OK. I mean, some places were quite cool, I suppose.'

'Like where?'

'We found an ammonite on a fossil walk in Lyme Regis.'

Ms Delauney's eyes narrow as she studies me, which she does a lot, like she's thinking about something all the time. 'You're lucky to have such a bohemian father. Not tied down to ideas of learning being confined to the rather restrictive walls of a school.'

'You think my dad's *bohemian?*' Her face doesn't change, a small inquisitive smile staying fixed there, so I just shrug. 'I thought he was pretty conventional . . . although I suppose I don't know him very well. Dad left me and Mum when I was really young.'

'Yes, well, that must be a difficult situation to deal with.' Her eyes flicker like she's confused, so maybe Dad told her something different.

We walk for a few more minutes until we reach a crossroads: three paths leading off in different directions.

'Which way?' I ask, although the path to the right is just a little rough track.

'Time to check, I think,' Ms Delauney says, swinging the small pouch on her hip round to the front and pulling out a crumpled map. She stretches it out so we can both study it, which is difficult because there are deep creases and lots of stains, some of which are blotting out important words, which makes me smile, although I bite the inside of my lip, so she doesn't see.

'It's that way,' I suggest, pointing at the rough track.

'Oh, well done.' Ms Delauney's voice has a little lift. 'You know, I've travelled the world, but I'm afraid I'm still rather hopeless at finding my way.' She smiles at me like she's sharing a secret. 'And I cannot abide Google Maps or smart phones.'

'My mum hated them too,' I tell her. 'I didn't even have one until recently.'

'Your mother was a sensible woman,' Ms Delauney says.

'Have you really travelled *the world*?'

She gives me a swift smile. 'Well, obviously, I haven't been *everywhere* there is to go, but in my younger anthropologist days I was quite an explorer.'

'Which places did you like the most?' I think about the enormous map that covered my wall in the house in Scotland. Mum didn't like travelling but I still liked looking at the pictures of pyramids in Egypt, and the Blue Mosque in Istanbul.

'Oh, every country is quite a mixture of things. Good and sometimes a little bad, but if I had to choose, I would lean towards India, which is so spiritual and beautiful.' She glances at me. 'Africa is quite wonderful too and, of course, was the beginning of so much that we consider civilised – writing, organised religion, even governments.' She gives a little laugh. 'Oh, but maybe I'm being greedy now . . .'

'I think they sound amazing places,' I say.

'My mother was from Jamaica. She left there in the 1950s and, even though she didn't talk about it often, when she did, I felt that I could hear the music and noises of the street and whistling of the breeze in the trees as if I were there.'

'So why did she leave?'

'Economic reasons. Wanting to "better" herself. Believing that she would feel at home in the Britain – the "Motherland" - she'd learned about since she was a child – but not realising that she would face rejection.'

'That's awful.'

She shakes her head. 'She had a good life in Britain eventually. And she met my dad, and they ended up with the house and the garden of her dreams and the entire neighbourhood would come round for wild, joyous parties every week . . . but I think I understand her more now.'

'What do you mean?'

'Well, she used to tell me and my sister folk stories about a character called Anancy but, much as we liked them, it was only later that I understood that they were little pieces of her homeland that she was passing onto us.' Her eyes are glowing and, for a second, she reminds me of Mum when she was telling a story, her hands wide and outstretched.

'Do you think that's why you're interested in myths? Because of all those stories your mum told you?' I ask.

'Do you know, no one has ever asked me that?' She glances at me. 'And I suppose the answer is that it probably is.'

'What are you researching now?' I ask.

'Well, I'm rather interested in spriggans.' Her voice

is a whisper. 'They were little scrunched up old men, so powerful that they could start sudden and horrific storms. People were terrified of them, although some think they were misunderstood and that they were just protecting burial sites, looking after the bodies and spirits of all our loved ones. That or the treasure that was buried there.'

'And what do *you* think?'

She pauses for a few seconds. 'I think they were jealous and attention seeking. Like difficult, wilful children suddenly given enormous power . . . You see, they also did things that were so horrifying that nothing compared.'

'Like what?'

Something about her eyes sends a little shiver through me. 'They stole babies from their cradles. And then they replaced them with a different baby. Except it wasn't really a *baby*. Just a shrivelled version of themselves . . .'

I watch Ms Delauney's feet as I walk beside her, still thinking about the spriggans and the babies, until I hear her wince each time her left foot touches the ground.

'Are you alright?' I ask.

She stops as we reach a cluster of boulders. 'I'm afraid I need to tend to my rather battered feet.'

'Do you need some help?' I ask when she winces again.

'I'm fine. I have a tendency towards blisters – which is not always conducive to long treks in the name of essential research.' She delves into her bag, retrieving a small medical tube.

'What's that?' I ask, suddenly spotting a stone hut fifty metres or so away.

Ms Delauney glances at it. The roof is sagging and looks as if it could fall in at any moment. 'Oh, some kind of disused animal dwelling, I would imagine,' she says dismissively, kicking off her shoes and socks, dabbing at her toes with ointment.

'I think I'll go and take a look,' I say, suddenly squeamish at the sight of the blood.

I walk towards the stone hut. It doesn't look that interesting but, just as I'm about to turn back, a noise makes me stop. I hunt around for an animal in the undergrowth but can't see anything. A few seconds later, I hear it again. It's a light tapping sound. And it's coming from the building. I edge closer, trying to work out the shapes through the windows. Until I can see more clearly.

It's a girl.

I stare at the window, wondering whether she can be real. Or whether she's like the girl I imagined at the house in Scotland. Mum laughed at me about it, but even now, I remember the feather-like touch of a hand on my hair.

But this girl seems real, and she waves – a tiny movement of her wrist.

I take a few steps forward, but suddenly she holds up her hand, warning me to stop.

And then she's gone.

I look at the empty window, waiting for a few seconds, but she doesn't come back. A shiver runs through me, and I race back over to Ms Delauney, who's leaning against the same jagged rock, studying the map, sipping water from a plaid flask.

'Did you see that girl?' I gasp.

'Sorry, I didn't .Was it someone else on the path?'

'No, I . . .' I start to say, but then I remember the way the girl held up her hand, like she was warning me. 'No,' I say quickly. 'I mean, it must just have been a rambler behind the hut.' I know I'm not making much sense and Ms Delauney glances at me quizzically as she packs up her things. 'I think we should head back before it gets dark.'

'Alright,' I say, looking over at the hut but I can't see anyone there now.

I want to say something all the way to the hostel, but I don't in the end, pretending to focus on the landscape, silent except for the pattern of our steps synchronising in steady, quiet thuds.

'I think you seem rather in your element outdoors,' says Ms Delauney when we are nearly back.

'I do prefer being outside.'

'Is it the air, do you think?'

'Maybe,' I say, shrugging. 'That or the colours . . . I mean, it's different inside. Everything seems artificial and washed out . . .'

'And this winter will come to an end soon and then the flowers will emerge, and the sky will be blue.'

'It's at the edges of blue now,' I say without thinking, seeing the twinkles of light on the sea in the distance.

'What colour would you describe it as?' she asks with a small, curious smile.

I hesitate, suddenly embarrassed, wishing I'd just said that it was 'pale blue' like a normal person. 'It's white,' I say, 'with some cornflower blue and a few wisps of grey . . .'

'What about the sea?'

'It's lots of colours,' I say, glancing at her to see if she's being serious.

'How wonderful that you see things in such detail.' She's smiling, so at least she thinks it's a good thing and not weird. But then I think of the girl in the hut again and shudder.

'Did you see something back there at the hut?' Ms Delauney can definitely tell that something is up.

'No,' I say, although I can't look at her. If she sees my

face she'll be able to tell that I'm lying. And I never lie. Or at least I never *used* to lie.

'Sometimes I have a sense of something that seems almost otherworldly, out here on the heath,' Ms Delauney says. 'It probably sounds strange, but sometimes I need to get the feeling of the earth and the air to understand the world in which these myths and stories were conceived.'

I open my mouth to tell her about the girl, but then I clamp it shut. It's something about the way the girl looked at me, her eyes massive with fear. But she wasn't a ghost or spirit. She looked solid. Real and breathing. And scared.

A little shiver runs through me. The girl must be in danger. And I know I must help her. I just don't know how.

Chapter Five

Clover

I can't sleep. My head has been whirring all evening, thinking about Mum and Dad. And the girl on the heath. I need to distract myself so, even though it's nearly midnight, I turn on my side light and creep over to the wardrobe, pulling out a stack of pages from the box. I crawl back into my bed, wrapping myself in a blanket and read Ruby's letter.

January 21st, 1851
Dear Aunt Iris,

Thank you for your last letter. I cannot tell you how much I love receiving them. Sometimes I can hear your voice clear as a bell. With Benjamin out all day, and Mama and Papa talking non-stop about all the amazing things they have planned for him – like grand universities and travel to Europe, where he will punt down rivers and sit on pavement cafés sipping French and Italian coffee – I feel as though I could disappear altogether, and no one would notice!

There is a new girl here. She is about my age, her name is Mary, and she works in the kitchens with Tildy. She appeared on the doorstep out of nowhere one morning in January. I spotted the hideous patteroller at the end of the drive and immediately realised why she didn't like me too much. I waved him away just as soon as I could although he tried to stare me down. I didn't care much. I detested him anyway. And he held his rifle with a great deal too much pride.

Anyway, I so hope that Mary will be my friend, although she has not said much to me yet. She is also the only person who is almost close to my age. I think I stared at her for a long time before I could string even a few words together, which now makes me blush some. I am determined to make her like me and even though she will not smile at me, I still like her. She has big eyes with long lashes and a sweet, fixed mouth.

Please write soon. Papa says you are very busy with all your abolitionist meetings, although, and please forgive my ignorance, I don't quite know what that means.

Your loving niece,
Ruby

I read the letter again, a prickle of irritation with Ruby working its way through me but it's only when I read it the second time that I properly register the words: *Abolitionist meetings*. It seems strange. Ruby's father owned a plantation, but her aunt was an *abolitionist*.

I had read all of the letters before. Countless times. At the beginning of the road trip, I often went to bed early. It seemed better than sitting with Dad for hours struggling to come up with conversation so I'd go to my room and read the letters, hoping that they might give me some clues about Mum. And why she had so many secrets. But, for some reason, I hadn't really thought properly about the fact that Iris was an abolitionist. And what that really meant.

There wasn't much in any of the school history worksheets about slavery or colonialism. But I do remember one day, when Mum and I were painting, Mum's face pulled and strained as she sketched a cluster of flowers from the garden and listened to a radio programme. I don't remember it all but there was something about how British plantation owners made lots of money in the Caribbean, because the people who worked all day, making them richer, were enslaved. The more I heard, the more I felt sick. People working in the fields under a blazing sun, whipped for the smallest thing, just so people in England could eat sugar.

'I'm so glad that doesn't happen anymore,' I'd said. 'Imagine eating sugar, knowing that.'

But Mum pursed her lips and shook her head. 'But what happened to all that money? It's still here. Still dividing the rich and poor.'

I didn't know what she meant, and I didn't like the look on her face – angry and confused – so I just carried on painting.

I lie back down on my bed, staring at the ceiling. I must have nodded off at some point, but when I wake up, the thoughts are still spinning round in my brain.

It's just before seven when I go downstairs for breakfast, a scent of orange marmalade and faintly burnt toast coming from the dining room. Ms Delauney is already there, lost in whatever she's writing by the window, streaks of sunshine bursting in and over her face so that she looks too bright, almost unreal.

'Ms Delauney,' I say quietly, not sure if she's seen me. 'Ms Delauney,' I say again, not wanting to disturb her but not knowing how to leave now I'm at her elbow.

She smiles, adjusting her glasses. 'You're up early,' she says before her eyes narrow slightly. 'What is it?' she asks quietly.

For a second, I freeze. It was Mum's secret box, after

all. But I can't work any of it out, and Ms Delauney knows a lot about history and places. 'Here,' I mutter, placing the little piece of fabric in front of Ms Delauney before I can change my mind. 'I found it,' I try to explain. 'I mean, after she died . . . It was Mum's.' Ms Delauney gently touches the cloth at its edges. 'It was in her box of secret things.' I say. I want to tell her more, but I can't explain that, after she died, I'd wandered around the house, opening every drawer, because I was trying to find something to cling on to that might make me feel better. I knew the heavy box under her bed was supposed to be secret, but I thought it wouldn't matter. Because Mum was dead, and nothing could change that.

But now I wish I hadn't seen the dusty pages of letters and the photographs of sweetly smiling parents and an older woman holding a baby in her arms who I think must have been me. And a small boy with fluffy, scruffy hair, and a girl with eyes the shape of lemon sherbets – who I recognised as Mum. Because the Mum I thought I knew now seems different. And everything I thought was true seems like a lie.

I must have zoned out but when I look up, Ms Delauney is still studying the fabric. She lays it down on the table, staring so hard at the pattern, that I wonder what she can be seeing. 'It looks somehow familiar,' she eventually says. 'Can I keep it for a day or two?'

'Yes,' I say, although a bit of me does not want to let it out of my sight. She rips a few pieces of paper from her writing pad, wrapping the fabric back in the tissue and then in the paper, as if it were incredibly delicate or precious.

'I have a few friends. Historians and anthropologists.' She smiles. 'When you are old like me and have led something of an itinerant existence, you often accumulate friends in different, and sometimes useful, places. This might well be an heirloom, or, better still, it might capture a piece of history that we don't know anything about. It's rather like a fascinating piece of a jigsaw puzzle, isn't it?'

I nod, slowly. 'It's just . . . Mum kept this fabric in a box, and she always said that it was her *one secret place*.' I can feel my lip quivering because I hate that memory. Mum's face forever frozen with anger, and disappointment, because she caught me, snooping around one day when the rain was pelting down.

'It's OK, Clover,' Ms Delauney says, lightly touching my hand. 'You're allowed to be curious.'

I finish my schoolwork at 1.30 p.m. Dad's still upstairs, making work phone calls that I don't really understand except that it's something to do with finance.

I need to go and see if the girl is alright, so I pack an overcoat, a bottle of water, a small sketch pad and some pencils into a small rucksack. I don't want Dad to stop me going, so I message to tell him I'm heading out for a walk.

The heath is moss green with tinges of brown, almost like it's burnt, except for a few dots of colour. It will be dark by five, so I walk quickly, and soon the dwelling appears in the distance, so battered it reminds me of a witch's hut.

A little shiver runs through me as I get closer. The land is so silent that I wonder if I'd imagined seeing the girl, but I still wait, hidden behind a bush a few metres away. The ground is damp, so I sit on my raincoat, trying to distract myself from the cold by studying the plants near my feet. I've been there for at least thirty minutes when I hear small, rhythmic sounds of footsteps coming towards me so I sink back into the bushes, prickles sticking into my back, and pull my legs as far in as I can. It's definitely someone small, but my nails are still digging into the palms of my hands when the sound stops a few metres away.

When I dare to look up, the girl is standing right there. She has long hair, which is mousy in colour except for a reddish tinge, and her eyes are the colour of damp leaves in late summer. She makes me think of a fairy – her wrists and hands bony, a small oval face with a little pointed chin and wide-set, unblinking eyes. Maybe an *angry* fairy, though, or a Tinkerbell – mischievous and jealous . . .

'Hello,' the girl says, the pursed, tight look on her face softening. 'Would you like some water?' She offers me a bottle.

'I've got some,' I say, reddening, 'but thank you, anyway.'

'What are you doing out here?' She suddenly doesn't seem very friendly.

'Walking,' I say, as confidently as I can, although there's a quake in my voice.

'You usually only get ramblers out here, marching on with their maps and compasses, not really looking at anything,' she says dismissively, which makes me laugh. 'What's your name?' the girl asks. She has an accent, although I can't work out where she's from.

'Clover,' I say.

'So, how old are you, Clover?'

'Thirteen,' I say, not liking the way she says my name, like she's mocking me or something. 'Nearly fourteen. How old are *you*, then?' I ask, suddenly irritated. None of the girls or boys at the school looked at me like that. They were scary in big numbers, when I couldn't work out who was saying what, but they tried to be kind at least.

'Nearly *fifteen*.' She looks younger. 'My name's Caterina,' she says jerking around at a sudden sound from the small building. 'I have to go,' she whispers.

'Can't you stay for a few minutes even?' I ask.

'Caterina!' a man calls out gruffly in the distance.

'Who's that?!' I ask.

Caterina just shakes her head. 'I thought he'd be out for longer,' she says. 'Come here again,' she urges, her eyes opening wide. 'But you mustn't let anyone see you.'

'But who's that man?' I ask. 'He seems sort of angry.'

She gives a brisk, decisive shake of her head. 'He's OK.' She looks at me and, for a second I think she's going to tell me why she's there, but she doesn't. 'And you can't tell *anyone* you saw me.' She studies me for a few seconds and then runs off in little light sprints, towards the dilapidated hut. After a few seconds, I risk peering around the bushes and see a man with a stern face and cropped hair at the door. I lean back into the hedge. My heart is racing but I don't know what to do. I want to run back to the hostel, but then I think of Caterina, and her bony arms and legs, living in the middle of nowhere. I need to at least see if she's alright.

I glance at my phone. It's late but I can't leave now. Not until I'm sure that Caterina is alright. I don't know what to do and now Caterina's gone it feels strange to be hanging around. I reach into my duffel bag, pulling out the sketch book and pencils, trying to do *anything* to stop the horrible pounding in my chest. Drawing usually helps me to feel calm. Some days when Mum was in bed all morning, the door open but her eyes to the ceiling, I tiptoed around the rooms of our cottage. They led one into the other, and I'd go around in a whole circle, feet on the cold stone floors as I opened cupboards and the fridge trying to find food to make the churning in my stomach go away. Sometimes, if there wasn't anything to eat, I'd walk into the fields, the long grass tickling the backs of my knees, until I discovered a patch of smooth grass where I could sit for hours, scratching at the paper until I'd sketched out some kind of shape. Or I'd watch a butterfly gently flapping its wings as it hovered by a tall yellow flower, until, eventually, that fluttering in the wings and my hands rested.

I look around, trying to find something to draw until I notice a cluster of flowers, bursting into pink and white spheres. I sketch them in swift strokes, shading them over and over to get the right colour, the right shapes and vividness until I lose my sense of time, and the tense feeling in my chest goes away. I exhale, long and slow, and put down my pencils, risking peering round the hedge again. I can't see anything at first but then I notice a movement and I see Caterina, at the window, lifting her hand in a small wave. I do a thumbs up sign to her, hoping she'll understand what I'm asking. She does a thumbs up back but I'm still not sure until she flashes me a smile.

I pack up my pencils and paper, calmer, but still with a sick feeling in my stomach as I slowly tramp back to the hostel. All the places Ms Delauney pointed out in the heath don't seem as magical anymore, because there's something not right with Caterina. I just don't know what to do about it and I can't shake the feeling that I might make it even worse.

Dad's in the living room area when I get back, sitting on one of the sofas, his laptop and a newspaper spread out on the coffee table in front of him. He's pretending to read, but I see him glance around every few seconds. 'You've been out a long time,' he says when he sees me, his voice strained.

'Not that long,' I mutter, although I can't look at his

face because I don't want to see that hurt in his eyes.

'Where were you?'

'Walking.'

'Where?' Little spider lines are at the corner of his eyes.

'The heath.' For some reason I still can't look right at him. 'I messaged.'

'You can't walk on the heath on your own.' His eyes are stern. There's no flicker to them. They're just like stones.

'I used to walk wherever I wanted in Scotland.' I glance at my phone. The message didn't send. 'I must have lost the signal,' I say, holding out my phone to show him. I want him to just leave it, especially as I'm already worried and upset because I can't stop thinking about Caterina and wondering if I should have done more. The way she looked at me when she told me to keep quiet made me uncertain. And she seemed so serious.

'Look, Clove,' he says. I roll my eyes. He's not going to let this drop. 'I get that this is difficult, and I know you've had a lot of freedom.' *Freedom.* That isn't exactly how I would describe being abandoned those days whilst Mum slept all morning. 'But you absolutely can't do that. If you try to go off again and not tell me or call or whatever then we're going to have a serious rethink of the rules.' Something makes me really irritated. Like he's suddenly this reasonable, responsible father, when he's ignored me for years.

'What rules?' The horrible, tense feeling in my stomach comes back and I feel hot and sick all at once, although I don't know why exactly. 'Why would you care anyway?' I ask, feeling rage rising in me so that I know my face is red.

'What do you mean?'

'You didn't know what I was doing for years. Why does it suddenly matter now?' As soon as I say it, I wish I hadn't. Although I've wanted to say it for months. Ever since he turned up to collect me from the house in Scotland. A man I couldn't even remember who was pretending to care about me all of a sudden.

For a few seconds he just stares at me, but then I catch a little flash of something in his eyes, like a streak of pain. 'Of course, I care.' Something about his voice makes some of the anger go away. He seems so sad.

He clears his throat. 'Anyway, do you want anything? Tea? Hot chocolate – are you cold?' I think about going upstairs and lying in my bed, but it won't help me to stop thinking about Caterina, so I end up saying yes and sitting on the sofa while Dad goes to the kitchen.

He comes back after a few minutes, with a steaming mug of tea. I grip onto it, trying to warm my hands.

'You're shivering,' Dad says, handing me a blanket before he sits down opposite me.

'Thanks,' I say, pulling it over my legs. He's staring at me, a little line between his eyes. I think he's waiting for me to speak. 'So why didn't you see us for years?' I ask, eventually, hating the aggressive tone to my voice, but I can't help it.

'Your mum never spoke about it?' I expected him to be nervous, or angry, but he looks confused.

I swallow. 'No. It's another enormous secret that nobody talked about.'

'What do you mean, *another?*

I bite my lip and shake my head. I can't tell him about the box. It was Mum's secret, and I was snooping in places I shouldn't have. And I can't tell him about Caterina. She implied it would be dangerous if I told anyone. I don't know what the right thing to do is, and I don't want to make things even worse.

'Look, it's really complicated,' he says after a few

seconds. 'I wanted to stay with you, though.' His voice trembles. 'I wanted to stay with you *and* your mum, actually.' He looks down for few seconds and then back up at me. 'It's just . . . I had to go back to London. I had to find a job and look after my mother who was ill. It just didn't work out.'

'But *my* mum was ill.'

'I know . . .' He seems desperate. 'Clover, I never stopped thinking about you.' I stare at him, trying to understand. 'I just made a mistake,' he says. 'A stupid, massive mistake.'

'What does that mean?' I ask, still feeling angry and upset. 'A mistake is something you do like spilling a drink or forgetting to lock the house when you go out.' I have a sudden image of Mum doing those things in the few months before she died. Maybe she was ill then. Maybe I should have known she was ill. 'But it's not abandoning your only child for seven years.'

'I know,' he says. I wait for him to say something that will help me to understand, watching as he clenches and unclenches his hands. But he just looks at me, a layer of moisture in his eyes. 'I'm so sorry Clover. I just can't explain. You just have to trust that I loved you.'

'But you'll tell me one day,' I say. I don't know if it's a question or a statement. He doesn't answer but stands up and goes to the kitchen.

'I'll make us something to eat,' he says.

Tea is awkward. We talk about schoolwork. And the weather, which seems ridiculous, and then play two rounds of cards. As soon as I can, I tell Dad I'm heading to bed. He sighs quietly. 'I can read you a story if you like,' he offers.

'I'm a bit too old for that now,' I point out.

'I used to read to you, though. Do you remember that?'

I shake my head but there are sounds in my head. It's not him reading to me but the night before Dad left. I cried under the covers, trying to ignore the angry voices downstairs. And that echoing word in Dad's voice: 'Please . . .'

'You used to tell me a story about a magician,' I say quickly, remembering, but wanting the memory to go away.

Dad's eyes and mouth don't move but his eyes fill with tears as he nods.

Chapter Six

Mary

February, 1851
Dear R,

Most days are pretty much the same. Ruby comes marching into the kitchen after her lessons when things are all chaotic with pots and pans and we are making bread in the stifling heat. She doesn't notice as she hangs around, complaining about her tutor. I don't say it, but I know how much Tildy would give for Martha to have even one single hour of those lessons on literature, mathematics or those far-off places that seem like a whole other world.

At least she's not like Adeline Bolt. Adeline had a mean, twisted-up face and could be all over the place – sometimes your friend then turn on you for the slightest thing. But just as I think maybe it's not so bad for Ruby to be there, chattering on with her face all pulled down, she fixes her eyes on me and asks if I will go with her to her room.

I glance at Tildy, my heart beating wildly with panic because I don't want to end up being turned inside out like with Adeline, but Tildy speaks without skipping a beat. 'Mary has a lot of chores to do with me in the kitchen.' She catches my eye but I just shrug. 'Maybe another day,' Tildy says, which makes my heart start beating again at least. 'But anyhow, child, aren't you supposed to be doing some reading or schoolwork or something?'

'I'm supposed to be doing whatever it is that is considered appropriate for a young lady,' she says. 'Which means not much at all . . . not like Benjamin's learning.'

'Now, Miss Ruby, you go back up to your room and do some reading and a little writing,' Tildy says. 'You know your momma and papa want you to learn good . . .'

'Do they?' Ruby asks, so quick I nearly like her.

'Mary can come another day,' Tildy says. 'When we're not so busy here with all these cornbreads and chickens to stuff.'

'Alright, Tildy,' Ruby says, smiling so much her eyes sparkle and she marches on over to Tildy and wraps her arms around her, tight like Martha does most nights. I think Tildy won't like it because she's told me time after time in her upright, proud way: 'I'm sensible enough to keep my proper place', although sometimes she adds. 'Sometimes makes me so mad I think I might boil on over.' But Tildy opens her arms and puts them around Miss Ruby, a small smile on her mouth until she properly opens her face and flashes a broad, shining smile.

'Do you think it would be considered proper for me to go with Ruby?' I whisper later, while we're making bread. I know how to knead it well, stretching it thinner and thinner until it's so wide and long that I need to fold it over and over. I like the sensation of the dough, the flour warm and soft, and at least I can think about my story inside and imagine different places when I'm doing that.

Tildy's standing over at the high table as she scatters in herbs and mixes them with swift movements like a figure of eight. 'Miss Ruby?' she asks almost absent-mindedly. 'Well, she's a bit spoiled at times, but she's sweet too. Got a bit of fire in her, like my Martha, but that's not such a bad thing.'

Martha is five years older than me. Some days she looks out for me, almost like I'm a little sister, though when I watch her tilt her head onto Tildy's shoulder evening times on the porch with the fiddle playing and the stars twinkling, I wonder how she can be so generous as to share her with me. Rachel is in her twenties too. Tildy says that most plantation owners would have married her off by now, made to produce more children to work on his plantation. Martha too.

'But there are no young men except Jeremiah. And he's already married,' I say.

Tildy purses her lips so tight I think it must hurt. 'Don't always matter,' she says, glancing at me. 'You take care mind,' she adds with a stern look.

I think about the fact that I don't know who my proper daddy is. Pete was loving and caring and kind until he and Momma were led off in chains, but I knew he wasn't my actual daddy. And Momma would never tell me for definite who was.

'Don't matter how nice Benjamin pretend to treat you,' Rachel hisses, coming into the kitchen to fetch some grain and water for the chickens. 'Just keep your distance from him.'

Rachel works with Martha most of the time. Rachel mostly looks after the chickens. Martha tends to the gardens. She can make anything grow. Sometimes I think she might be talking to the plants, encouraging them to bring out their colour although they reckon it's harder work than the kitchens even though on a hot day you think you'll burn alive. Rachel likes the chickens at least. They make her smile as they peck at her ankles, and she knows each one. 'Tildy,' I asked one time, 'what's wrong with Rachel's leg?' She isn't mean but she doesn't speak to me that much. She's all cheekbones and proud face. And she doesn't walk right.

'Tried to run away about four or five years ago. Them patterollers just as mean as you can imagine. They don't care what they do.' Tildy pauses, a little flash of pain in her eyes. 'They say she was running away, and they had no choice, but they beat her leg real bad. Beat her leg and drag her behind a horse for hours, like she just a sack or something.'

Some nights, lying on the hard floor, crammed into the cabin with my toes so close to Rachel's they touch, I think I hear her sigh and wince in pain. One time when it's hot, Martha silently takes over her blanket, folds it to make a cushion and puts it under her foot.

Most nights, I wait until everyone is asleep and go into my story inside. I imagine I'm in a field full of flowers, lying on my back as I stare at the sky and watch the clouds nudging each other along, while music fills the air, a piano tinkling like a chorus of angels. And Reuben is there, listening for the crickets, and their buzzing, chirping sound crawls its way into my ears at night.

Sometimes I think I hear the voices of the babies too. Distant and soft, their whispers like song alongside the birds on the indigo night air. Momma nearly died trying to get him out. I saw him. Perfect, as Momma cradled him in her arms, small droplets of tears falling onto his arms and face until she wiped them away. And he just looked beautiful. And still.

Sometimes I just lie there, listening to the rustling of the trees on the roof of the cabin and think about Momma. And dream that I'm free, running in the fields. With big open skies.

But then I'm caught and dragged behind a horse.

Chapter Seven

Clover

'The fabric comes from a quilt,' Ms Delauney tells me when I come down for breakfast. Dad is on a business call. I heard him pacing around his room for at least twenty minutes, his voice rising every once in a while. 'The designs were special, like a code, and this particular pattern, the triangles, was intended to convey a message.'

'What kind of message?' I ask, my heart beating a little faster, thinking about Mary and Ruby's letters and all the things I don't understand.

'Well, there's a theory that these quilts were used by an organisation known as the Underground Railroad to help runaways to reach freedom. They were hung outside houses to convey different messages depending upon the design.' She taps the fabric. 'This symbol is flying geese, which meant to travel north.'

'Birds?' I didn't tell Ms Delauney but, whenever I looked at the pattern and lines, I thought of birds. Usually, I couldn't see whatever it was that Mum saw in things. I even caught her wincing, once or twice, when she asked me what I saw in abstract patterns of lines and markings, sensing her eyes fixed on me. I knew that she wanted me to say something creative or imaginative and to not be too *technical* or something.

'So, the fabric *is* special?'

'It certainly is,' Ms Delauney says, with a little satisfied nod of her head.

I had hoped it was. Not just because it had been in the box, but because Mum obviously loved it so much. But a little stab of pain makes me frown at the memory of a day last spring. One of my favourite memories, but also one of my *least* favourite, which is how lots of memories of Mum seem to be at the moment. The top of the stable door's open and there's a flash of powder blue curtains floating – I'm drawing or colouring in triangles or diamonds, some strange geometric design, anyway, and Mum is painting a magnolia in an amazing colour. 'I love your painting!' I say and then I show Mum my picture.

'Like birds,' she says, nodding approvingly. But it *wasn't* birds. At least, I hadn't meant it to be. I just liked the shapes and the colours and the way everything fitted together.

'What's troubling you, Clover?' asks Ms Delauney.

'It just doesn't quite seem like *her*. I mean, why would she keep the fabric in a box under the bed? Why didn't she take it to an antiques dealer and tell me the story behind it? Mum loved that kind of thing . . .'

'I don't know,' she says, wrapping the fabric up in the tissue paper. 'Clover,' she says, her eyes focused on the tissue paper, like she's thinking about what to say. 'Maybe this is something you and your father could share? Maybe *he* knows about the fabric – about the story behind it.'

'What could he know?' I blurt out.

'Well,' she says slowly, 'they did know each other for quite a long time.'

But not for the last seven or eight years – not since he left me when I was only six. And Mum and Dad hated each other at the end . . .

'I don't know if I want to hear all the bad stuff,' I say. 'I mean, all the arguments and things. All the reasons why they couldn't stay together . . .'

'Of course not,' Ms Delauney says. 'But he also knew her *before* that. Before all the arguments.'

My mind's whirring, trying to work out what I *actually* know about *them* – like how they met, where they lived and what they did before me . . . And I'm blank. So maybe Ms Delauney's right.

'Clover,' she says softly. 'I think you have every right to be angry.'

'About what?'

'About whatever you want to be angry at . . .' But then she looks at me. 'But don't you think your dad loved your mother once? That maybe he's a bit sad too?'

'No,' I say, because I don't want to think about that, but I blush. Because it's a lie. I heard Dad on the phone. Lots of times – to the psychologist, and to the school, trying to discuss things in a calm, even tone, often so quietly that I struggled to make out any words. But I still heard my name – and Mum's. And I also saw his face when he'd come back to the living room, trying to hide his eyes. 'So, shall we go to get pizza?' he'd suggest with a lift to his voice.

But his eyes were red and puffy. And deep. Like wells all filled up with sadness.

And his face reminded me of me.

Chapter Eight

Ruby

March 5th, 1851
Dear Aunt Iris,
Benjamin would scold me for writing again so soon and say that I am being too demanding, but I really don't know who else to tell all these things to and, for the last few weeks, everything seems quite strange. Even Benjamin seems a little changed and my vile tutor, Mr Thistlewood, is becoming more sour and cross, if that is possible. He growls at me if I dare to have an opinion and refuses to teach me most of the things that Benjamin does at school because he says such learning is not 'appropriate' for young ladies.

Mary has been here for eight weeks now. I still don't seem able to persuade her to trust me. And Tildy won't let me help in the kitchen, although I may well be quite useless as I cannot cook a thing. It still hurts though when she shakes her head, her lips pursed tight. Today she looked at me and said in a quiet voice, 'No one choose to do this.'

Iris, I'll have to stop this here as I am being called down for dinner by Mama who will fret if I am late. Benjamin would be able to smooth her with his smile, but he has been forced to stay with one of the boys from school for what is likely to be a dreadful birthday party. After breakfast, Benjamin whispered to me that he hoped there wasn't going to be any hunting. Plenty of the boys seem to think that shooting defenceless animals is fun so there probably will be hunting of some kind and Benjamin will hate it and not be able to forget it for days on end.

Please write and tell me about your work. Everything here is so dull and small. I long to hear about important things and to feel like there is something going on in the world.

Love,
Ruby

March 16th, 1851
My Dearest Ruby,

I was delighted to receive your letter. Please never apologise. I am, as you suggest, much occupied with work during the day but in the evening myself and my dear friend Charlotte return to our rooms and are sometimes quite lost for entertainment. I am always glad to receive one of your letters, though I do feel somewhat saddened by your obvious loneliness.

I am afraid my uses here are currently quite limited. However, Charlotte and I are determined to become better acquainted with the law so that we might become a little useful. We recently had an exciting visit from a woman called Josephine Herbert, who was active in efforts to bring about the abolition of slavery in British territories in the Caribbean. It seems to have been a long and difficult road despite the immense passion of many of the abolitionists. Josephine Herbert, a woman who is now quite elderly but still carries herself with dignity, advised us that the abolition of slavery was only achieved because the plantation owners were paid enormous sums of money in compensation for what they deemed to be their 'property'. Money with which they became immensely rich.

I hope that in time I can contribute more. I believe that our voices can be our greatest means of bringing change. Indeed, I have very recently learned first-hand the power of our words. Last Thursday I met a very interesting man, Robert Morris. He is a young lawyer of colour who, born a freeman, was appointed as a servant in the home of the eminent lawyer, Ellis Grey Loring. Young Robert Morris studied the law and is now using those skills to seek to right many of the wrongs that are committed daily against people of colour. Today I heard that he recently represented a man whose former enslavers tried to steal him back from freedom under the barbaric new Fugitive Slave Bill.

Continue to write. Continue to admire the flowers that grow in the lovely corners of the plantations. Continue to think about the world, dear Ruby.

Your loving aunt,
Iris

Chapter Nine

Clover

I read Iris's last letter again, especially the part when she talks about the campaign for the abolition of slavery in the Caribbean. I think about that day when Mum and I heard that radio programme and Mum said something about how it was still affecting people. I search around for my phone, googling 'slavery in the Caribbean and compensation'. When I find the information, I have to read it twice.

Approximately £20 million was paid to the plantation owners in compensation for their freed slaves. It was an enormous sum at the time and repayments for those loans were not paid off until 2015.

It seems unbelievable. And so wrong – that the money was paid to the *plantation* owners and not to the people who were enslaved. I take out my notebook, scribbling down a few words: *abolition, compensation, Fugitive Slave Bill*.

But when I put the letters away in the box, my heart is beating fast. I can't breathe and it feels like something's around my neck. Pulling and tightening.

I don't know what it is. All I know is that I need to do

something because it's feels like being strangled. Iris felt like that too. Like she was seeing something terrible yet not doing anything about it.

It makes me think of Caterina.

As soon as Dad's in a meeting, I head off to the hut. It seems too quiet, though. Everything is completely silent except for the sound of small animals in the dry twigs of the nearby bushes, but I still wait, my knees pulled up and my back flat against the hedge so that no one can see me. After about ten minutes I get my drawing pencils and sketch book out, trying to distract myself by focusing on a cluster of trees a few metres away as I sketch out the lines and the leaves. Every few minutes I poke my head outside my little safety zone to see if anyone else is around. On the fourth time, I see the man walking away from the hut. For some reason I focus on his feet and his clunky shoes as he strides purposefully, not taking my eyes off him until he's so far away that he seems to merge into a landscape of rock and heath and sky.

As soon as he's gone, I hear a girl humming. I know it's Caterina but the little flutter of excitement in my chest stops when I remember how she was the last time I saw her and how unfriendly she seemed. But, before I can change my mind, I see her, clambering over a clump of rocks towards me.

'Hello,' she says, stopping still in surprise. 'I was coming for water,' she explains, holding up three empty bottles. 'There's a stream. We don't have any water in the place.'

'Oh,' I say.

'We're not supposed to be staying here,' she says, her voice rising slightly, 'so you can't say anything.' She looks at me, and her eyes narrow. 'I'm guessing you don't have many friends, though,' she says.

'What's that supposed to mean?!' I'm more irritated than stung by the comment and start gathering together my pencils.

'What's that?' Caterina asks, pointing to my sketch pad, her eyes suddenly wide. If she knows she's offended me she doesn't show it.

'Just some drawings,' I say, putting the pencil tin back in my bag.

'Can I see?' she asks, her voice suddenly softer.

'OK.' I hesitate as I hand over the book. I don't want her to look at the drawings and think they're childish or pathetic, but she studies each page, turning it around to look from different angles.

'Wow!' she says eventually.

'Thanks,' I say, sensing a little flush of pleasure.

'You sound surprised,' she says. 'And you're blushing.' I take back the pad. 'Sorry. I mean, they're good. Really good,' Caterina says. 'Anyway, do you want to walk with me?'

'OK,' I say. I'm confused by the way she changes but Caterina nods in a vague direction and I follow her, noticing her long strides even though she's so thin.

'Are you *alright*?' I ask quietly, biting my lip. 'I mean, that man looks a bit scary.'

'He just gets worried,' she says, shrugging.

When we reach the stream, Caterina hands me one of the bottles to fill, taking a few handfuls of the clear water and wiping her face roughly.

'Do you use this for washing as well?' I ask.

'I told you we didn't have any water,' she says with an irritated scowl. 'Anyway, what do you do all day if you're not at school?'

'Art. Schoolwork . . . I go for walks. Here, or near the hostel.'

'That's where you live? That big old house over there?' Caterina points in the direction of the trail that leads back to town.'

'Well, not *live*, exactly, but we're staying there . . . My mum died, and my dad thought a road trip, as he calls it, was a good idea.'

'Doesn't your dad have to work?' she asks.

'Well, he *does* work.' I sound defensive, although I'm not sure why. 'When I'm doing my schoolwork. And sometimes at night.' In fact, he works at night a *lot*. Even last night I woke at 2 a.m. and heard him padding around his room, then tap-tapping on his computer keyboard.

'So, have you been anywhere good yet on this road trip? Or just *here*?' Caterina asks. Something about the way she waves her arms around, and the little sneer when she says 'here' makes me laugh.

'I like it.'

'That's because you're an *artist*.' I look at her for a few seconds trying to work out if she means it. 'I have to go back now,' she says, suddenly nervous, although she reaches out and touches my arm. 'I'm really sorry about that no friends comment, by the way . . .'

'Don't worry,' I say.

Caterina gives such a wide smile that she seems almost like a different person. She's still looking at me intensely, which makes me blush, but there's also a fizzing feeling in my stomach. Until I notice how much her cheekbones seem to be protruding. Like she's even thinner than before.

'Do you *need* anything?' I ask. 'I mean, clothes? Or food?'

'Not *clothes*,' she says, biting her lip. 'He'll notice

clothes . . . But food is good.'

'I can help you. Maybe my dad could help too,' I say.

Immediately Caterina's face changes and she looks fierce, her eyes burning into me. 'If you tell anyone I'll kill you . . .' she says, which makes me flinch. 'Well, not *kill* you exactly, but just *please* don't. It's important.'

'OK,' I say, still shocked.

'It's just, if they catch us, they'll definitely kill us . . .' she whispers, her green eyes enormous and unblinking. 'Or maybe something worse.'

She walks away, her arms swinging, not even glancing around before she reaches the hut. I watch her go through the door, but she doesn't turn back. She just closes it quickly behind her, leaving me with lots of questions, and a sense that this has happened before, that this is somehow an echo of something I can't quite place. But as I run back towards the hostel, all I think about is, who is she? *And what can possibly be worse than being killed?*

'Are you alright, Clove?' Dad asks that evening in the middle of playing cards. We started playing Gin Rummy early on into the road trip. At the beginning, every day at breakfast, Dad tried to discuss a plan for the day. After the first few days he stopped asking because I just glared at him because I didn't want to think about what to do, and I definitely didn't want to get to know him. I just wanted my mum back. So we cycled around the New Forest and went on a fossil hunt in Lyme Regis, but the evenings were still awkward until Dad got out a pack of cards. 'Clover?' Dad shuffles the pack, his eyes focused on his hands. 'Are you OK?'

'Yes.' I still haven't told him about the box. Or Caterina.

Dad takes a sip of coffee, a tiny frown above his eyes.

I want to tell him about Caterina. She's obviously in

danger and Dad might know what to do at least, but an image of her scared face shoots into my head. What if Caterina's right? What if she could get killed? So I keep my mouth shut.

Dad deals the cards out. I can tell he's disappointed. It doesn't usually bother me but for some reason this time it feels horrible.

'I looked in Mum's box,' I say quickly. 'The secret one she kept under her bed.'

'Oh?' He glances at me but then looks back down at the cards.

'You know about the box?' I ask, watching Dad's reaction. 'I know I shouldn't have looked in it,' I say.

'It's alright, Clover . . .' His voice is so soft I think I might cry.

'There were photos of Mum and her parents . . . and these ancient letters from two girls in America – Mary and Ruby. I've no idea why.' I try to control the quake in my voice. 'And I found a piece of material, about this size.' I stretch out my hands, making a square with sides the length of my handspan. 'Ms Delauney says it comes from a piece of a quilt and that the patterns are symbols that helped people escape from the plantations.' His eyes slightly narrow but he doesn't look annoyed. Just like he's listening, which makes me carry on talking. 'Why would Mum have that? And why don't I know who those people in the letters and photos are?' I stop, a sudden horrible, acidic taste in my mouth.

Dad doesn't say anything. He just puts down the cards and looks at me. 'Your mum's mum – your grandmother – used to write a lot of letters.'

I swallow. I can't tell him that I read one of her letters. That I've read it five or six times, wondering how Mum could ignore her. And, almost worse, how she could have stopped me from knowing her.

'Mum said I didn't have any relatives. That it was just her and me and we had to be enough for each other . . .' Dad winces. 'Which is ridiculous. I mean, what with the fact that she was lying to me about it, and perhaps just about everything.' Before I can stop them, my eyes well up with tears, and even though I wipe them away, they keep falling down my face. 'Maybe she was even lying when she said she loved me . . .'

'Clover,' Dad gasps. I think he might hug me, but he just takes my hand, grasping it in his large warm palm, twice the size of mine.

'Dad,' I say when I can speak properly again. 'I literally can't stop thinking about it and wondering what she was hiding . . .' My head's fizzing. All I know is that I'm annoyed at Mum, which I hate. 'It's not even about the quilt . . . well, not *only* that.' I swallow, trying to keep my voice steady. 'There are just so many things that I don't know.' There's a little flash of pain in his eyes.

'Dad, I need to find out,' I say, and my voice cracks.

'What, about the box? The fabric?'

'Yes,' I say. 'And about Mum too,' I add.

He takes an inward breath. 'Of course,' he says quietly and then he looks at me, almost excited. 'Why don't we go somewhere that she liked?' he asks.

'What, like around here?' I ask, confused. 'She knew this area?'

'Yes,' he says. 'It was one of her favourites.' He glances at me. 'It's partly why I thought we should come here on this road trip . . .' He gives a little laugh, like he's embarrassed. 'It sounds a bit simplistic now but it's why I thought you might like it too.'

* * *

I go to bed at ten. I tell Dad I want to read, but I really want to read Grandma's letter again, hidden in the pages of the book on my bedside table.

Dear Sara,

We think about you all the time. We had the photograph album out this evening. Dad found it hard to look at the photos but, for some reason, that picture of you on your first day of secondary school comforts me in some small way. It reminds me of why we are in this situation. You have that look of determination and conviction on your face. Like you are so certain. I always admired you for it. You knew what you wanted and what was important to you. So, in some way I understand. But, Sara, I want you to know that we are doing everything we can to explore the history of the company. I don't want to enjoy its profits if it was not made honestly and decently. You must believe that.

In the meantime, look after yourself. And please look after our dear Clover. We have her photo on the mantelpiece. We often recall memories of her, talking about how sweet and honest and funny she can be. And how curious.

Even if you won't see us or speak to us, will you consider letting us get to know Clover again?

Please keep yourselves well. We love you.

Mum

Chapter Ten

Mary

April, 1851
Dear R,

It's spring now. The plantation is edged with magnolias in full bloom, their branches draped in pink and white. Not just dots of blossom but perfect, beautiful flowers on each branch stretched out like long limbs.

I sit beside Tildy on the step, trying to take a few breaths of air before we go back inside. We already scrubbed the floors. It took so long I thought my knees would crack. Tildy scrubbed so hard that when I looked at her, she seemed angry and like she was in another world, until she stood up, wincing as she rubbed her back for a few seconds.

We have an hour before we start preparing for dinner but it's so hot that we sit outside. I'm peeling potatoes into a bowl when I see Rachel scattering grain for the chickens. 'Why did she run away, anyhow?' I ask Tildy. 'The Finch folk seem nicer that the Bolts.'

Tildy's voice is cold and strange when she answers. 'Don't matter what sort of place this is, still trapped here. You know we're all on a list of their chattels, like we're just property? When Martha was born, I promised myself she'd have a *different life. Know what it is to run in the fields, maybe get herself a little education.'* She glances at me, lowering her voice to a whisper. *'Even got me a plan to escape.'*

'What happened then, Tildy? Why didn't you get away?' I asked.

'First time, the plan went wrong somehow. No idea why but no one showed up.' She sighs. 'That was at Massa Donnelly's.' I look at Tildy, waiting for her to carry on, but she inhales suddenly, her breathing heavier than normal, her face frozen and her eyes big and staring. I jump to my feet, sprinting to the kitchen to get the chestnut leaves, that Martha always dries until they are perfect, from the small wooden box. I add a few of the precious leaves to hot water, bringing the tea back over to Tildy, which she sips while I rub her back.

'Why didn't you try again, though?' I ask gently, once Tildy can speak again.

'Had another baby,' she says. 'Called him Gabriel, after the angel. But the pain was awful. I knew something was wrong.' For a moment, Tildy stays completely still. 'Sometimes I wonder whether it's the Lord's way. Make sure nothing going to force my baby away from me, a boy baby that Massa Donnelly would have been quick as anything to make sure went on the block soon as he was able, sold off to any old evil high bidder that come along . . .'

'So, what happened?'

'Massa Donnelly needed money quick. So, he sold me and, thank goodness, my Martha too.' She pauses. 'Mr Finch just about decent enough to make sure he bought both of us. Plenty of others happy to stand by stone deaf to the screams of a mother wrenched away from her child.'

'And this is better?' I ask.

'Mary, this heaps better . . . but don't matter how decent Mr Finch is compared to other folks, he still thinks it's just fine *to enslave living, breathing, feeling folk.' I watch as she looks off at a place in the sky. 'And there ain't a single day when I don't see Benjamin go off to school and not feel something like hatred that my Martha with her brains bigger than her head don't get that opportunity – trapped in this life, working in fields . . . Hurts so much I want to scream.'*

That night, I dream of Momma. Sitting on the porch singing. Her voice is low and full, and she can hold a note so pure and clean for longer than I can hold my breath. 'You need to follow the north star,' she says, her voice cutting through the darkness. 'That's all I know. Better learn your way, when you get out of here.' Her eyes are fierce as she adds, 'I just long to be able to picture you somewhere in the green and air on the horizon.'

And when I wake up, I wonder how I could have forgotten.

Chapter Eleven

Clover

'What will your clients do if you are out all day exploring?' I ask. It's two days after Dad promised he'd show me somewhere that Mum liked.

Dad gives an impish smile. 'Catch up tomorrow,' he says.

We drive for thirty minutes. Dad has his playlist on most of the way. I don't mind until he plays a folk track by Sandy Denny, and I have to hold my breath. Mum played it a lot, streaks of paint on her hands as she sang along, her voice so clear it reminded me of a songbird.

We reach a car park high above a town. 'What are we doing in St Ives again?' I ask, getting out of the car.

'It's somewhere your mum liked,' he says simply.

'OK,' I say, trying to smile but I can't. I know I asked him but, now we're here, I don't know if I can cope with thinking about Mum and all the places she liked.

But after a few minutes, I quite like it and we're just walking. Dad's not constantly telling me which roads and paths they walked on, or anything like that. We are just wandering around and it's actually nice, being somewhere different, and I like the whitewashed houses and cobbled streets lined with coloured cottages in pastel blues and yellows.

The sun is shining through the clouds when we reach the sea, the golden sand contrasting with the colour of the water. 'Mesquite,' Mum would have said, although it's really a dull grey-green, but I still like it, dotted with the tiny colourful boats on the horizon.

'You hungry?' asks Dad. 'Is it too early for chips on the seafront?'

'No,' I say, laughing, 'and lots of salt and vinegar, please.'

'Saw a seal here once,' Dad says as we sit on a wall at the harbour, hot chips in paper on our laps. 'Your mum took off her shoes and waded into the water.' There's a hint of a smile on his face, the edges of his mouth just lifting, although his eyes seem somewhere far off, trapped in a memory.

'How did you meet?' I ask.

'University halls. At Exeter. She came up to me. I thought she was this beautiful, ethereal creature with hair the colour of chestnuts,' he laughs, 'and she had all these clothes on . . .'

'What's *that* mean?!'

'I mean, they were *flowing*, I suppose.' He blushes. 'Well, you know – long skirts and long dresses and lots of hair. Everything just, you know, *flowed*.'

'She loved floaty skirts,' I say, suddenly remembering Mum in a long purple skirt made of crepe when I was little. I'd shouted, 'Turn around again!' And she whirled around, her skirt forming a circle. 'So what did she say?'

'She said that, even though I was evidently a scientist or an engineer – something *solid* is how she described it – she wondered whether I'd be interested in going to watch her play Ophelia.'

'She was just trying to sell tickets? That was the only reason she spoke to you?'

'Yes,' he says, a smile crossing his face.

'That's not very romantic . . .'

'I know.'

'And did you go?'

'Of course. And it was magical. *She* was magical.'

'She was right, though,' I say. 'You *were* doing one of those types of subjects.'

'Yep,' he answers, shrugging his shoulders with a little impish grin. 'Yes, I suppose . . .' He smiles, a broad smile that stretches across his face. He looks happy.

But I suddenly feel something's hurtling towards me, a heavy weight of a rock in my chest that won't lift and go away.

'You weren't solid for me, though,' I say, immediately wishing I could unsay it.

Dad doesn't say anything after that. He just gathers together the papers and puts them in the bin. 'Walk?' He suggests, creases all around his eyes.

'OK,' I say, following him. His shoulders are hunched, and I wish I could bring back the way he'd looked when he told me about Mum. But I don't say anything. I just walk a few metres behind him, along the coastal path, lined by flowers just beginning to emerge into colour.

'Shall we go on the beach?' I ask, spotting the steep path down.

'Of course,' Dad says.

I stop to take off my shoes and, by the time I step onto the cool sand, Dad's smiling again as the water runs in small rivulets over his feet.

'Look, Clover,' he says, handing me a small purple stone. It's beautiful and smooth. 'It's like some exotic treasure,' he says. He reminds me of a fisherman, with his bristling dark beard, worn skin and crinkled, bright eyes.

'I like stones,' I say, gripping it and turning it over in my hand.

Dad crouches down, drawing lines in the sand. 'You liked stones even when you were little. You used to paint leaves and rocks. You loved the colours,' he says, 'and the shapes.'

'You remember that?'

'Of course, I do.'

I kneel down, a metre or so away from him. I feel like I'm in a trance as I let my hand brush over the grains, creating grooves in the sand. I can't look at him. I don't want him to see my face. 'Mum didn't really like my paintings,' I say. I try to make my voice light, but I can't.

'Why not?'

'She said they were too *accurate*.' Mum's leaf and flower paintings were always more vivid, embellished in ways that made the collection of leaves seem very ordinary as they lay on the large pine table, browning and curling with air and time.

'What is it?' I ask suddenly seeing Dad's face, which seems twisted and tense.

'It doesn't mean that you're not good at something . . .' he says, his voice quiet. 'Just that you do it *differently*.' He touches my shoulder, a light feather. This time I don't flinch, and it doesn't even feel strange so that there's a little sinking in my heart when he takes his hand away.

Chapter Twelve

Mary

May, 1851
Dear R,

The sun's streaming through the window as Tildy pounds the dough at the table, fist tightly clenched. Ruby's standing at the door of the kitchen, a wrinkle hovering in a crooked, spidery line above her eyes. 'Tildy,' she says in a voice so quiet it's a whisper. 'You said that Mary might come and spend time with me.' She gives a little smile at the end, which ends up in a flash of energy.

I've been here long enough that I'm used to Ruby now and the way she hangs round the kitchen, trying to help with the cornbread or the grits, although Tildy always shakes her head. I'm now sure that she's not like Adeline Bolt at least. I tip my head down for a second, thinking about that awful day when I was ten or eleven. It's like a knife cutting into my chest all over again. I thought Adeline was my friend.

'Was this the child who did it?' her momma asked as we stood on the porch.

I watched her, waiting for her to tell the truth, but Adeline looked me in the eye and nodded. 'She stole your brooch, Momma, not me.'

For a few seconds I was fixed to the spot. As if I had no breath left in me and then panic and rage took over and I cried out, 'I didn't! I didn't, Adeline – you know I didn't!'

It didn't work. When her momma went out to get a long lash, she didn't even flinch. But as she lifted her arm, I saw Momma, from the corner of my eye, running towards us, eyes ablaze. 'Don't you do that to my child!' she screamed out.

When she reached us, she looked Miss Clarissa Bolt full in the face. 'If Mary says she didn't take the brooch, then she didn't,' she said.

But Clarissa Bolt didn't even blink. 'You'd obviously prefer to take the lashings yourself,' she said.

That was the first time I saw Momma like that, gritting her teeth as much as she could until a scream came from her mouth.

I looked for anything I could find, the magnolia on the branches of the tree, or a bird resting on its nest, anything to shut out those cries.

But I'll never ever shut out Adeline's face, her mouth, not moving or twitching as the blood trickled down Momma's back.

'Mary.' Ruby jerks me out of the horrible memory of Adeline and my momma and those thoughts in which love and pain always seemed to be tied up together. 'Are you alright? You looked like you weren't quite here for a moment.' She laughs, and the sound is a wind chime on the porch in the breeze.

'Well, Miss Ruby, you better ask Mary if she'd like to go with you,' Tildy says without so much as glancing up from the dough she's kneading. I try to catch her eye before looking back at Ruby until eventually Tildy notices and nods.

'I'd like to go,' I say slowly, holding my breath.

Ruby's beam gets wider as she leads me along the hallway towards the sweeping staircase. When we reach the top, we pass three doors until Ruby stops and opens the one to her room. Inside is all frills and lace, and on top of a shelf is a big doll in a yellow dress and little bonnet all by itself.

Ruby looks at me, following my eyes to the doll. 'Here, hold her,' she says, taking it from the shelf. The yellow dress has ruffles and little satin bows. 'You can have it if you want,' she says, tossing her head. 'I don't like it much anyway. I prefer building, or art. Making things.' She shows me a stack of small wooden bricks. 'I can make all different things – bridges, whole towns,' she says. 'I know they might look a bit babyish, but I can balance them so that I get the bridges just right. Benjamin says it takes real mathematical skill.'

I look at the doll, feeling that softness round its middle and the heavy, perfect china head that looks as though it will break if I don't hold her perfectly still, but I force myself to shake my head. 'What would your folks say?'

She shrugs and puts the doll back on the shelf, pulling a book down instead. 'This is my favourite,' she says, showing me a hard-backed book with colourful pictures on every page.

'Can you read those words?' I ask but she laughs, which makes me blush, although she clasps my hand and smiles in a way Adeline Bolt never did.

'Of course, I can read the words,' she says, hitching up her skirt a few inches before she lies face down on the floor with the book in front of her.

She beckons me over and I sit beside her, watching as she turns the pages, colours merging in and out of each other. But when she turns the page to a picture of an ocean I gasp. Little pieces of light reflect in the waves against a stretch of white-yellow, tinged by the sun. 'I've never seen the sea,' I say.

'We went to the coast last year. We paddled in the water and walked on the beach.' She looks thoughtful for a moment. *'It was really nice.'*

'What is this book called?' I ask, looking back at the words and the front cover.

'It's just a children's atlas,' she says. *'It's probably too young for me but I like thinking about different places and imagining exploring them.'* She glances at me. *'Look, I'll teach you,'* she says, as if it's the easiest thing in the world, taking my hand as she points to each letter. She traces the path of an 'S' telling me to think of a snake. I think of the snake slithering in our cabin a few weeks ago, before Rachel threw a knife at it and it darted under the gap of the door, leaving the knife lodged so hard in the floor that it took three people to try to pull it out.

'I can remember that,' I say, impatient to discover what the other lines and marks mean.

'Well, the others aren't quite so easy,' she says. *'But this one is an "i" – just think of it as a little person – a stick person with a little head on the top. Well, sort of . . .'* She laughs, a little ripple which makes me smile. She shows me a 'z', telling me it's like a zigzag shape and an 'l' that she says is like a line. *'This says Switzerland. It's a country,'* she explains. I nod, not really knowing why, but feeling as though a whole other world is being revealed, like going through a secret door.

'Ruby.' I hadn't heard anything but it's Benjamin standing in the doorway, his face like storm clouds. I think he must be annoyed about Ruby lying on the floor, or because I'm there, but he just pushes the door closed behind him, so quietly that the click is just a tiny sound. *'You have to be careful,'* he says to Ruby, sitting down on the other side of her.

'About what?' Ruby asks, shooting him an evil stare.

'It's illegal,' he says. 'Enslaved people can't learn to read.'

'No one has to know about it . . . goody two shoes,' she says, which make his cheeks catch fire.

'It's not that. It's just . . . it's dangerous,' he says. He doesn't look at me, but I watch him out of the corner of my left eye, noticing his wide-set eyes and a tuft of mid-brown hair swept to one side. But then he shrugs. 'I won't tell anyone.' He moves closer to Ruby, who nudges him and gives him a massive smile, which makes me think of Reuben.

That night, lying in bed in the pitch black, the moon a new sliver and not enough to reach in and light up the corners of the cabin, I write a different part to my story, words flying about my head. And, in my story inside, I pull down a book from a high shelf, and walk right into places like Japan and Switzerland, with snow-topped mountains and houses made of paper, and different flowers and trees scattered along the mountains and insects scrabbling around in the earth. 'Look, Mary,' Reuben says, 'Watch how it moves, how it searches around testing the safety of the place.'

I listen to the whistling of owls in the distance, the gentle wind carried in through the window and the crickets in the distance chirruping. And then I think of Benjamin and his soft smile and feel the little beat that my heart does, a little rush in my veins, until I remember Adeline Bolt and it stamps out like a smothered flame.

Chapter Thirteen

Clover

I haven't seen Caterina for three days. Since the day in St Ives, it seems more difficult. Dad is just *there* more often, which is sort of nice, but I have to think of all kinds of reasons to disappear or why I might be back late. And yesterday, when Dad had to go back to his house in Hampshire, it was obvious he'd asked Ms Delauney to 'babysit' and she came up with loads of plans, which was nice but also made it even more difficult to get away.

I scribble out a note for Dad, leaving it with Ms Delauney before breakfast. She gives me a small, quizzical look, but I just say that I'm going for a walk.

I reach the hut by eight o'clock, hiding behind the bush a few metres away. It's over forty minutes before I hear the creaking of the door and the light, brisk footsteps of Caterina.

'Hello,' I say, when she appears around the hedge. But Caterina's face is all scrunched up into a scowl.

'What is it?' I ask.

She doesn't answer at first, her eyes hidden beneath a swathe of long hair which hangs over the left side of her face. She sits down on a rock, pushing her hair roughly behind her ears and focusing her eyes on me. 'What did your mum die of?' she asks quietly.

'Cancer,' I say, strangely relieved by the directness of her question, though wondering what made her ask. 'She didn't do anything about it in time and then she collapsed one day and never came back home.' My voice quakes on the last word and I suddenly feel light-headed and have to stop speaking. I stare down at my feet taking short, deep breaths of air. 'Here, I brought some food,' I say, digging deep into my bag and pulling out a small loaf of bread, a carton of juice, a few tins, packets of biscuits and a bag of apples.

'Thank you,' Caterina says grabbing a piece of bread which she rams into her mouth.

'What made you ask that?' I ask, partly because I hate watching Caterina gobbling food. She's obviously starving, but if I suggest helping her again, I think she might get angry. Or even worse, refuse to see me.

'I was sitting here thinking about my mother,' she says. 'But I don't want to talk about her.' She shakes her head, seizing one of the apples and taking big bites. 'Thank you,' she gasps through mouthfuls. I don't say anything, waiting for her to finish.

'Do you think your dad was sad that she died?' she asks.

'Yes,' I say. 'I think he might still be sad.' I think about his wide smile when he talked about her being 'ethereal'. But then a little shiver shoots through me, and I remember Mum at the hospital, lost in tubes and chemicals. And the constant beeps of machines.

'That's good,' Caterina says.

'What do you mean?'

'Because then you have someone to share that with. Those memories of her.'

* * *

I run the whole way but I'm at least half an hour late for Dad. I knew I didn't have enough time to see Caterina, but I couldn't sleep thinking about how hungry and cold she must be, so I had to at least try. When I reach town, I see Dad sipping earl grey tea, the pages of a newspaper opened up wide. He glances around the cafe every time he takes a sip of his tea, and, for a moment, I just watch until he rubs his eyes and stares out of the wide, bright window towards the grey-blue sea.

'Hello,' I say, walking over to the table, surprised at how relieved I am when he smiles, and I don't have to see that sad expression anymore. 'I'm sorry.'

A large mug of hot chocolate is on the table in front of my seat. 'It's still warm,' he says.

'What was Hampshire like?'

'Good,' he says. 'It was useful, anyway. I needed to sort out a few business things . . . so did you get out with Ms Delauney?'

'Yes,' I say. 'We went for a walk. She's still researching myths for her book.'

'Anything interesting?'

'It's *all* interesting . . .' I look at him. 'So, was that all you did? Just *business* stuff?'

He smiles. 'Mostly.'

I lift the mug of hot chocolate up, holding it in front of my face so I don't have to look at him. 'I thought you might have looked for some other stuff.'

'Like what?'

'I'm not sure,' I say, shrugging, not quite able to explain my suspicion that his sudden trip had something to do with Mum. And all our questions. All *my* questions.

'Well, I did find *some* things,' he says, drawing out his words.

'Like what?'

'Well, I wanted to look back through some papers and old letters. I wanted to get it right . . .'

'What do you mean?'

He puts down his drink, turning his chair slightly towards me. 'Well, it's quite a long story . . .' His voice is strangely quiet. 'But the short version is that your mum's parents owned – still own as far as I know – a successful department store in London.'

'What, like Selfridges or Harrods?'

'Well, not quite that size, but substantial, nonetheless. Anyway, it was started by their grandparents, and a few years ago a newspaper did an article on the business. They said it was founded on the profits of slavery.'

I shudder. 'What do you mean?' I think about Mum's comment about things still being affected in Britain.

'Because the founder of the business, your great-*great*-grandfather, came to London in the late 1850s or 1860s. But it turned out that he came from a family who owned a plantation in Georgia in the USA.' He swallows. 'They had over thirty enslaved people working on the estate.'

Georgia. So, that was why Mum was so interested in the letters. Although, I still don't exactly know why she had them.'

'Wait, who was the founder?'

'Someone called Benjamin Finch.'

Benjamin Finch . . . A little shiver runs through me. But it makes sense as well. Ruby talked about his plans to go to Europe and travel.

'What is it?' Dad asks. 'Have you heard of him?'

I nod, thinking about Tildy's comment about him being 'turned around' by the world.

'So, the papers thought it was immoral?'

'Yes, and your mum was horrified. She cut all ties with her family. She said she didn't want to be associated with a family whose children received private education and privileged opportunities on the back of such misery and inequality . . . She felt their wealth was tainted.'

'Well, if he used his family's money for his business, then it *was*,' I say, a little too loudly.

'Yes. Of course. All these big businesses and grand homes need to look at their history and take some responsibility . . .' There's a little throbbing in his left cheek, a tiny little movement, almost like a little shiver, or tremor. 'Except . . .' He pauses. 'She didn't wait to find out the whole story. She didn't wait until her parents had explored the claims themselves. She just rejected her family instead . . .'

I think about the letter from my grandma and how she said they were 'exploring' the history of the business. 'But *did* they do anything?' I ask, suddenly not sure what I want the answer to be.

'As far as I can tell, they did a proper investigation.'

'Did Mum know this?' I feel sick. 'I read bits of those letters from my grandmother – I mean, not *all* of them. I mean, I didn't *want* to read them all . . .'

'Because they seemed too personal?'

I nod. 'So maybe she didn't have to cut them off?' I'm suddenly irritated. 'And then maybe I would have grandparents, at least. And cousins or something.' I'm not just irritated. I'm upset.

'Let's go to the beach,' Dad says quietly. 'It looks sunny now.'

'OK,' I say, slowly standing up because I want to get outside. I want to walk and get rid of this horrible feeling.

It's cold outside, even though the sun is bright, but we

go onto the beach and the yellow sand feels nice and soft under my feet.

'I get that you're angry,' Dad says.

'I'm not really sure how I feel,' I say, crouching down to pick up a bright shell which is smooth and black and purple inside even though the outside seems ordinary. 'I love this beach.'

'I love *all* beaches,' says Dad, smiling. 'Well, not crowded beaches with sunbathers in front of high-rise grey concrete buildings. But ones like this. Sometimes it feels like you're the only people on earth who realise how precious this is, to be standing on the sand in winter or early spring. With this air. And light.'

'Can't you move to a house by the sea?' I ask.

Dad doesn't answer. He just carries on running his fingers through the sand, creating deep lines with his fingers. 'Maybe it's time we thought about where to live,' he says, a hint of a question in his voice.

'What, *now?*' My heart starts racing. I don't want to leave yet. What about Caterina? And Ms Delauney?

'Not until you're ready.'

'Do I get a say then?' I ask, turning to him.

'Of course, you do.'

As we walk along the beach, my head's still all over the place and there's something jagging at my brain even though I try to shut it out.

'Clover,' Dad says, his voice low. 'Your grandma lives in Winchester.'

I look out towards the sea, clutching the stone. 'Really?' I say eventually, my heart beating, faster and faster. *Dad knows her address.*

'Are you alright?' Dad says, gripping my elbow.

'Yes, I'm OK.' I try to nod but my heart's beating wildly.

'Let's walk back. It's pretty cold.' Dad's hand is still on my elbow, which feels comforting but strange too. Maybe I'd forgotten how it felt to be touched. Mum had been so different. She was exuberant and affectionate. 'Cuddles time!' she'd shout, chasing me around the room. I would laugh, my head thrown back, until she caught me and then she'd fold her arms around me, and we'd sit together like that for minutes – hours even. Laughing at an old Cary Grant film that I didn't always understand even though I still liked his smile; his strange, clipped voice and fake annoyance.

'How do you feel?' Dad says as we head back to the hostel.

'Angry,' I say. 'And I don't like that feeling.'

'That's alright,' he says.

'Dad, it wasn't just because the letters were personal that I didn't read all of them . . . I just didn't want to remember Mum in that way. Like she could be cruel.'

'That's OK, Clover. Whatever you feel is OK.' Dad's arm brushes mine as we walk up the tiny lane fringed by tall yellow flowers.

'Dad.'

'What is it?' he asks quietly.

'It's not just that . . . It isn't just what I think of her. It's what she thought of me.'

'What do you mean?' Dad asks, looking at me sharply.

'I didn't always think I was how Mum wanted me to be. She was all free and wild and artistic. And I don't think I was how she expected, or wanted, me to be all the time.'

Dad bites his lip. 'But she still loved you more than anything,' he says eventually.

'I know,' I say. 'I just wondered if . . .well, maybe I'm more like *you*.'

I can't tell if he's pleased or surprised, a strange half-smile flashing across his face.

But then I spoil it again, even though I know it's cruel, 'And that confuses me more,' I say, 'because you left me.'

It's nearly eleven at night. I'm lying flat on my bed, thinking about Mary and Ruby and Mum when there's a knock on the door.

'Night, Clovie,' Dad says, gently opening the door.

'They must all be connected, don't you think?' I blurt out. 'The piece of fabric and my grandparents' business?'

He nods, although he seems distracted.

'Maybe we could find out about it,' I say, 'through the internet or the library or something . . . Ms Delauney says she knows people who are experts in American history.'

Dad still doesn't say anything. He just stands awkwardly at the door.

'What is it?' I ask, suddenly worried as he pulls something out of his pocket.

'I found this at the house.' He hands me a letter. 'It doesn't explain everything. Not really. It was all very messy and difficult and even I can't remember the ins and outs well enough to trust myself to tell them properly, but I wrote this to you the evening after I left. I just never sent it.'

'Do you want me to read it now?' I ask, feeling a little sick. I don't want to do it in front of him, where he can watch every reaction.

'Read it if and when you like,' he says, 'it's not urgent. It's just . . . I wanted you to know.' He shifts again, for a moment looking as if he might say something, and then he closes the door.

After he's left, I look at the letter.

Dear Clover, it says.

Dad's side of things . . . It makes my stomach do strange little flips, so I put the letter back in the envelope, still sensing that tightness in my chest. Because what if it makes all the good things about Mum disappear? Her big smile and the way she'd wrap her arms around me, kissing my face loads of times?

I didn't tell Dad, but yesterday, when Ms Delauney and I had gone for a walk, there was a moment when the sun was drenching our faces and Ms Delauney had stretched her arms out. 'Spring. Renewal,' she'd said dramatically, crouching down to study some yellow flowers bursting with colour by a rock. 'Just imagine a world without these little bits of drama on the hillside,' she said, 'or the foreboding colours of the sky, or pink blossom in spring.'

'That's the sort of thing my mum would have said,' I said without thinking.

'I think your mother sounds like my kind of person,' she said.

'I'm not sure Mum *would* have been your kind of person exactly,' I said, worrying that I was betraying Mum again. But they were so different. Ms Delauney was so disciplined, always up at 6 a.m., positioned at the window with her notebooks laid out neatly beside peppermint tea, the scent drifting around her, like she was in an efficient, refreshing bubble.

'She wasn't very organised, I mean.'

But Ms Delauney smiled. 'Your mother seems to have been rather marvellous.'

I don't know why but a little ripple of joy rose up in me, tears pricking my eyes, so that all I could think of to say was, 'Thank you.'

And now all I can think is that I don't want that to

change. So, I put the envelope away in the box, underneath the pile of photographs and letters, and shut the lid.

Chapter Fourteen

Mary

May, 1850
Dear R,

The first time I go to my story inside, Momma was whipped for something Adeline Bolt lied about to her momma. The second time, Ned was caught.

No one tried to run away from the Bolt place. And no one came in, apart from those awful speculators. Except for one time.

After Ned escaped there was a sort of hush. A few days later, the bell rang out long and loud when we were out in the fields and, when we trudged back to the yard, we knew it was a terrible sign.

I didn't see Ned at first. Just those paddyrolls on their horses, mean and proud as they looked down on us. And then I saw him, tied up so tight his wrists bled and face drooped down like he'd gone out of his body.

Massa Bolt made us stand there and watch as Ned was strapped to a tree, his face flat against that rough bark so that I knew he would be scratched and cut to pieces, his arms fastened tight around it. They took a long curling whip and *beat his back until it was covered in wide red stripes. I felt sick. And I wanted to scream out to the skies, but I kept my eyes focused on Ned, and made my mind go somewhere far away. So I turned myself inside out and imagined I was high up above everything, carried on the wing of a bird. Sailing and floating, up and up above the fields and blood and pain.*

Chapter Fifteen

Clover

I stare up at the tree above me, the branches hanging over me like an umbrella while the forest-green leaves flicker and flutter about like a butterfly. I've been there for over half an hour and there's still no sign of Caterina. Usually I'd wait, but it's already half past nine and I promised Dad I wouldn't be long – so that we could get to Winchester.

I scribble out a note – *I managed to get a few things in town. See you soon* – along with a smiley face, folding it into four sections before I place it inside an old biscuit tin I found at the hostel. I put the few bits of food I managed to buy inside, some biscuits, two apples, a satsuma and a few cans, then I balance it against the base of the tree trunk, loosely covering it with a few damp twigs. I gather a few stones and pieces of bark nearby, making it into the shape of an arrow so she can find it, although I don't know if Caterina will see it, but then I remember her quick, sharp eyes and think that she'll notice every tiny thing that has even slightly changed.

But the knot in my stomach gets tighter as I start

walking back. Because last time I saw Caterina she was skinny and pale, but when I said to her that I could get help, she fixed her eyes on me so that they looked sunk back and scary and said, 'You don't want to turn up one day and find me dead do you?' So, I kept quiet, again. Still not sure if it was the right thing to do.

The office building is different from how I imagined. It's old, with faded red bricks and is on a cobbled side street full of small offices with elegant plaques. The woman behind the front desk has long black hair that gleams and she's wearing bright red lipstick. 'Follow me,' she says, smiling, although she looks at me a second or two longer before breaking into a wide, polished grin.

I study her feet as I walk behind her and Dad, the small heels of her boots tap-tapping on the wooden floor. 'This isn't the main office building,' she says, flinging open a door to a conference room. 'This is mainly for keeping documents, and doing some admin, but the proper office is at the store in London.' The room is painted a bland beige that Mum would have hated. There's a table in the centre of the room, but nothing else, and it's empty except for the large jug of water and gleaming glasses in the centre. 'Have you been to the store?' the woman asks.

I shake my head.

'You should. It's wonderful. All old-fashioned elegance . . . if you like that sort of thing, I suppose!' She smiles. 'Anyway, I'll get some coffee for you.'

'That would be very kind, thank you,' says Dad.

'Now, do you want anything else?' the woman asks, indicating the files. 'I'm Priya, by the way. All these documents are copies so don't worry if you spill something or whatever.' She walks out of the door.

Dad pushes over a small pile of papers to me, giving me a smile which looks like it's somewhere between an apology and excitement.

I look at the first page, but it just seems to be a list of documents, deeds and contracts and shipment records. Nothing about anything that seems to tie in with the letters. And nothing that I can connect to the shy boy hanging around the kitchen, or rich, spoilt Ruby. And definitely nothing about Mary. 'Here you go,' Priya says, coming back into the room with a tray a few minutes later. There's a rich aroma of coffee which, for a second, makes me jolt, reminding me of coffee and warm bread on a Saturday or Sunday in Scotland, which were usually good days, because it meant that Mum was feeling happy and energetic and wouldn't be lying on her bed for hours.

'It's a shame Sean isn't here today,' Priya says.

'He works here now?' asks Dad, his voice showing his surprise.

'He joined the business after his father died. Co-runs it with Mrs Harwood. His children are at school down the road so it's easy for him to come in after the school run.'

'I was always fond of Sean.'

'We all are,' Priya says simply, walking out of the room and gently closing the door behind her.

'Dad?' I ask. 'Who's Sean?'

'Your uncle,' he says. 'He was working in the city as far as I knew.'

'What, I have an uncle?' Dad nods. 'And cousins?'

'I think so,' Dad says, 'although I don't know much about then.' I can sense my heart beating fast and there's a little fizz of warmth in my stomach.

'Do you think they might be my age?' Cousins and an

uncle. And a Grandma. I had only ever had a Mum in the entire world. And an absent, distant memory of a dad.

There's another knock at the door. Priya hands two pieces of paper to me. 'Sorry, I forgot these,' she says. 'Ms Harwood – your grandma – thought you might find them interesting.'

They're photocopies of newspaper articles. One is a local investigative piece, printed in 2004, which I start reading even before Priya finishes closing the door.

> *In this new backlash against capitalism, many are questioning the origins and practices of those businesses and institutions occupying proud positions in our community and yet which have, at best, murky beginnings . . . Little is known about the man who founded the department store Iris. Many letters and documents were destroyed in an early fire but, what is known is that he was from a family that owned a plantation in Georgia just prior to the American Civil War, enriching themselves with the labour of over thirty enslaved people. It can only be questioned whether the foundations of this company were also based upon such immorally acquired profits . . .*

The other's an obituary, written in 1921.

> *Benjamin Finch's aunt was a pioneering, anti-slavery activist. Benjamin came to London in 1858, aged 25. He founded the treasured department store, Iris, in 1861. The business still thrives, occupying a proud place not only in our local community but in London. Known for his*

> *philanthropic works, including annual sums of money given to the local hospital in Alton, and much loved in the community, he is survived by his wife and three children.*

'It doesn't make sense,' I say, studying the blurry, black and white photograph. I look for clues – I'm not sure what exactly, but he has a kind, warm face and laughing eyes. 'The person described in the obituary doesn't seem like this evil man the journalist is referring to.'

Dad gives a wry little laugh. 'Well, maybe not *evil*, as you put it, but there are certainly a lot of questions . . .'

'But the obituary says he was philanthropic.'

'Maybe he did some good deeds but at the time of his death no one thought to question how he actually financed this business.' He shrugs. 'Anyway, how do you want to divide this up?'

I hand him a small pile of papers. Dad slowly works his way through his cafetiere of coffee, but one cup is enough to make me feel on edge, so I stick to the water, finishing the whole carafe because my throat is dry in the airconditioned room. I work through the list and all the files in the pile in front of me, but it's just monotonous documents and data forms with strange codes and numbers, and none of them seem to answer any questions.

'Whose are all the initials, do you think?' I ask after a while. 'I keep seeing two sets of initials. BMF must be Benjamin Finch but who is MCS?'

'I don't know . . .'

'What is it?' I ask Dad, whose finger is hovering on something.

'I'm not sure,' he says. 'There's something here, though. It's dated March 1860, just before the business got going.

A Mr Stemming-Stokes seems to have invested a sizeable chunk of money in the business.'

My head hurts and I massage my forehead, just above my eyes.

'Anyway, enough for today,' Dad says decidedly. I look at the clock. It's four thirty. We've been here over two hours. 'Are you alright?' he asks, and I nod.

On the way out, Priya points to a picture on the wall. It's heavy with an ornate metallic frame. It's a family tree, with beautiful, twirling writing in a dark brown ink. I look at the top of the tree, which traces back over two hundred years to 1760. 'They came from England?' I ask.

'Yes. As far as we can tell they didn't intend to rely on the labour of enslaved people when they first emigrated to America.'

'So why did they change their mind?'

Priya gives me a strange look. 'Because it was hard. And the labour was free. They realised they could make more money.'

I stare at her feeling sick. Priya gives me a sympathetic smile and then points to Benjamin Finch's name on the family tree. I follow the lines, leading through the generations towards my grandma, Evelyn Harwood and then my mum, Sara – and then to me.

'I thought it would be nice to have family,' I say to Dad as we make our way outside. 'I thought it would be great to feel like I belonged . . .'

Dad glances at me. 'But not to this family?'

'Not really,' I say. 'It's good that the business is called *Iris* though, don't you think?'

'Why?'

'Because Iris was Benjamin's aunt. She was an abolitionist.'

'There are a lot of good people in that family tree,

Clover.' Dad touches my arm. 'But anyway, all of this, and whatever we find or don't find isn't really about them or whatever terrible, or good, things they may have done. It's about what *you* do now that matters.'

We spend the night in a Bed and Breakfast in a cobbled street near Grandma's office. My room has a four-poster bed, and the floors are wooden. It looks expensive, although Dad says we got a 'deal' because it's out of season and midweek. Dad's reading a paper when I come down for breakfast the next morning. It's only 8.30 a.m. but he must have been up for a while because his cup's empty and there are pastry flakes on a plate.

'Thought I'd leave you to sleep,' he says.

'Did you look at anything else after you went to bed?' he asks, seeing my notebook.

'I read those other papers that Priya gave us,' I say. 'And I googled a lot . . .' Dad mock frowns. 'Just for an hour, to see if I could find out anything more.'

'OK,' Dad says. 'And did you?'

'Benjamin did apprenticeships in London before he started the business. When he started *Iris*, it was a tiny shop. Not this massive department store that it now is. . .' My voice trails off. 'I'm still confused about why Mum reacted the way she did. I mean, there's no evidence that Benjamin did anything wrong. He worked hard and didn't take money from his family. I don't get it . . .'

Dad shrugs. 'I'm not sure if she knew all the facts... and you know, your mum was not like you exactly. She was wonderful in many ways, but she was more instinctual.' I sense a little warmth in my stomach. Caterina had asked me if Dad was sad, and I thought he might be, but he never really said that she was wonderful before. Not like that. Not like it was just a fact, which feels nice, until I think about the word he used. *Instinctual*. It feels a bit like a stab in my chest again. Because I'm not like that - creative and expressive and artistic.

Dad frowns and folds his paper, placing it beside a small basket of golden croissants, the smell of fresh pastry and orange juice making me hungry. 'But yes, it does all seem above board . . .' His shoulders tense though, and I can see that his right hand is slightly clenched.' 'What is it?' I ask.

'The money from Mr Nicholas Stemming-Stokes . . . I looked him up.' He grimaces. 'His family owned a sugar plantation in the Caribbean in the late eighteenth century. There were over two hundred enslaved men, women and children on the plantation, working in terrible conditions. He was a very rich man. And, when slavery was finally abolished, Stemming-Stokes got even more money in payment for all those people who he'd forced to work for nothing on his plantation. Like they were just property. Things.' I can feel my face getting redder. 'It was three million pounds in today's money . . . Three million that he then invested in other businesses all over the country. Helping his family to grow their wealth.'

My heart sinks. 'I thought Benjamin wanted to change things.'

'Benjamin might have just made a mistake. And he wouldn't have known. They didn't have the internet and access to all the resources we do now. And the Stemming-Stokes family had lots of power and would have seemed upstanding to many of their peers.'

'Because of the money.'

'Yeah, I know,' Dad says.

I think about all those letters from Ruby and Iris.

'Benjamin should have known better than anyone that having money or influence didn't mean being good people.'

Dad doesn't say anything, and I stare at my drink as numbers go round in my head. When I finally glance up, he's looking at me.

'What's wrong?' I ask, my heart beating faster.

'I was wondering if you wanted to meet your grandma later?' Dad says.

'What, you mean today?' There's a weird mix of emotions battling in my head.

'What is it?' Dad asks suddenly.

'I don't know.' I can't tell him but, even though I want to meet her, it would remind me that Mum lied to me. And what if Grandma is nice? That would mean that, when she was sending all those pleading letters, Mum was ignoring her. It meant Mum could be cruel. I didn't want to think of her in that way, because then all those memories, the fairy picnics and the long walks, Mum showing me every flower and leaf and exclaiming at the magic of the world, and those gigantic, fierce hugs she gave me, would just seem fake too. Like fragments, or an echo of something that might have happened, but which no longer seems real.

'It's confusing,' Dad says.

'Sometimes, she seemed like the most amazing mother that anyone could have . . .'

'I know.'

I'd daydreamed about meeting my grandma, but now, it seems too much, and I stare down at my hands because everything feels like it's spinning.

'Next weekend, perhaps?' Dad offers, gently gripping my hand. 'It'll give you the chance to get used to the idea.'

'OK,' I say, although my mind's whirring with everything. And however much I go over it all in my head, I don't know what to think. And now it's not even just Mum and Dad. It's finding out about this whole family history. With its terrible secrets.

Chapter Sixteen

Mary

June, 1851
Dear R,
At first, it just seems like every other Sunday. We're given our passes so we can walk the two or three thousand paces along the dusty roads to the church in town. I don't mind. The church is shaded and cool and we get to walk slowly, past trailing wisteria flowers in mauve and purple, drooping over big, beautiful houses with their shaded porches and swing seats out front. And azaleas and rhododendrons dotting all those front gardens with colour, the scent seeping into the air, like an exotic honey.

We have to sit at the back of the church, but I love listening to the songs and Tildy's beautiful voice is rich and low like Momma's, the music echoing all around us in a warm circle.

Ruby smiles at me when she walks in, until her momma tugs her back round to face the front, not wanting all those white folk to think it's not proper, or some other fool thing, but Tildy nudges me because it's prayers. 'Close your eyes, Mary,' she whispers.

The sun is beating down when we get out of the church.

Women with lace-edged fans wave them in front of their faces and it's so hot that I find some shelter in the shade of a tree. I stand, watching the ants scrambling up and down the rough bark while I wait for Tildy and Martha, until something makes me turn around. At first, all I see is a wagon outside Mr Anderson's grocery store, but then I notice that, sitting in the front, hunched over like he's afraid of the world, is a small boy. Something about his hair and the way his body all bunches up tight is familiar and, when the boy moves, something shifts like light inside me. I run over the road, not stopping to look out for carriages and their horses. 'Reuben!' I scream out. 'Reuben!' I call again until I'm standing by the old cart I remember from Massa Bolt's, right in front of Reuben, looking at his eyes and hair and small downturned mouth for the first time in months.

'Mary,' he cries, reaching out his stick skinny arms.

Before I can even touch him, Mr Gore, the overseer, comes out of the store. 'Get yourself gone, girl,' Mr Gore shouts at me, his face creasing up and twisting with rage and hate. I know his eyes, deep and fixed in his rough and weather-worn face the colour of rust. I remember how he made Hannah jump over a whip, like it was a skipping rope, her feet so swollen she could barely move. His face stayed fixed in a broad, twisted smile and he used all his force to bring that whip down on her when she tripped over. He'd beaten Momma that time too, for not getting enough cotton even though she was eight months big with a baby in her belly.

A rage rises up in me. 'Can't tell me nothing now,' I say, looking him square in the eye.

He draws back his arm, clenching his hand into a fist, but then he stops, looking around angrily. 'Who dealing with this girl here? Who you belong to, girl? I get the slave catchers on you if you ain't got no pass,' he yells.

Reuben stands up in his seat, but Mr Gore slaps him down hard. Something about Reuben's eyes terrifies me – like he's forgotten all the stories and how to turn himself inside out so that no one can get to the delicate middle part. But Mr Gore whips the horse so that it races off, its sweating nostrils flaring as the cartwheels turn. 'Reuben!' I call out, a sob catching in my throat. 'You gotta keep going; you gotta remember your story inside!'

But it's too late.

I watch the cart drive off, my head throbbing, and see Mr Gore's whip is high in the air, and come down and strike Reuben across the face.

I think I must scream at the exact same moment Reuben wails, a strange echo on the air as if we are completely linked, two parts of the same person. But then I hear footsteps nearby and turn to see Tildy and Martha running towards me. 'Shhh, shh, child,' Tildy says, patting and stroking me. 'Calm down. Stop screaming, Mary, you've gotta stop screaming. Mr Finch may be better than some but he still a planter and don't like people talking about him and his business as much as anyone.'

But I'm crying so hard I don't think I can stop.

'Don't worry, she's calm now,' Tildy says. 'Just not feeling right . . .'

I glance around and see a whole wall of fans, parasols and waves of lace. Miss Rose Waverley, who Ruby always says is 'stuck up', mutters something about 'commotion'.

'Come on, Mary,' Martha says, gently tugging me back towards the road. I'm still crying but I walk with them, following the dusty path, as the houses start to disappear, between the fields high with wheat and cotton, until the Finch house comes into view.

I hang back, following a few paces behind. Martha

occasionally glances round to check on me, but I walk slowly, only vaguely aware of the heat and dust and flies buzzing around my face and landing on my shoulders so that I have to flick them away. All I can think about is Reuben's face . . .all those things I tried to close off, so that I could turn myself to stone, just to survive, come back to me. Like Momma and how she looked when she was taken away, and how, even though I knew her heart might break, she still held her head high as she tried not to allow her soul to be beaten down and to keep that little pocket of hope inside her.

But the reverend's words in the church keep going around in my head. 'We are all equal under God,' he said and all those people with their fans and glittering jewels around their necks and tall hats just sat there and listened and nodded . . .

It makes me sick.

'Mary.' It's Benjamin, appearing beside me, his mouth twitching with anger. 'Mary, was that your brother?'

I stare at Benjamin so hard he flinches, but he keeps his eyes locked on to mine even though I can tell he feels hurt. 'Mary,' he says. 'I'll ask my father to buy your brother.'

He winces at the word 'buy' but my heart surges. 'Please, Benjamin, please, please,' I whisper.

'It will be alright, Mary,' he says, as we walk into the plantation, through the gates.

'No, Benjamin. It won't be alright,' I say, staring at him. 'It won't ever be alright.'

'What do you mean?' he asks, but I just shake my head and walk off, sensing his eyes burning through my back.

Chapter Seventeen

Clover

The hostel is empty when I come down for breakfast. A group of ramblers have just left, and it seems quiet and lonely without the buzz of energy and chatter. Which seems strange. I always found noise difficult. The classroom at the school was claustrophobic and felt too much to cope with but now, as I sit in the echoing dining room, a half-eaten bowl of soggy cereal on the table in front of me, I wish there were more people around.

Dad's gone away again. Last night, after four rounds of cards, he announced that he was going somewhere on 'business'. I tried not to show it, but my mind started racing. At least I'd be able to see Caterina and wouldn't have to think of lies to Dad's ton of questions or his attempts to 'help' with my schoolwork when he doesn't have a clue about most of it.

But just as I'm working out a plan, and what food I can take, Dad mutters, 'Ms Delauney says she'll keep an eye on you.'

Ms Delauney takes it to a whole new level, dividing the day into segments which she tries to fill with 'mini adventures' as she calls them. After I finish my schoolwork, she suggests that we go to *Delicious Doris*, which is one of those teashops that sell cream teas and looks like it's out of a Jane Austen novel, which is why she likes it. I'm still worried about Caterina, but I force a smile. 'That sounds fun,' I say.

We sit in a window seat for three hours, drinking tea while we research myths, Ms Delauney writing detailed notes in a hard-backed exercise book that looks like it comes from the 1940s.

'This is rather civilised,' she says with a grin, as she spreads strawberry jam on the scone before adding the cream with a little flourish.

'Yes,' I say. I love talking to her and helping with her research, I just wish Caterina wasn't constantly on my mind.

'I'll need to credit you when I eventually finish this work,' Ms Delauney says. 'You really do have an eye for detail.'

'Thank you.' I smile at her but end up looking down because I'm sure I'm blushing. 'I mean, I don't seem to be good at that much.'

'That's what you think?' She arches an eyebrow. 'You mean school subjects?'

'Not just that, although going to school was hard. I was good at English but everything else was difficult.' Heather and Ayesha found science and mathematical problems easy, but I ended up staring blankly at the sheet. It made me feel stupid.

'You know, most things take time. For *everyone*.'

'Maybe.' I don't tell her but it's not even just school. I'm not good at anything else either. Like art. Or cooking. Or making friends.

'Clover.' A frown flickers across her eyes. 'You really

are *very* good at this research. I think you have rather an aptitude for it.' Ms Delauney pours out tea.

'Thank you,' I say but I can sense myself blushing so I look back at the newspaper article I've been reading: *Uncovering the Myths of the Mines*.

'Do you think we should actually visit a tin mine?' I suggest. 'You know, to find out more about the creatures they believed in – you know, like knockers.'

'What, sort of field research, you mean?'

'We could try speaking to some people who used to work in tin mines. Maybe they could tell us something about the spirits of the knockers that protected them or whatever it was they believed.' I glance at her. 'If that doesn't sound ridiculous . . .'

'I think it's an excellent idea. It will give a very human angle to the story – and I'd personally be fascinated. Some local people come from generations of miners so, even if they have more conventional views, they may have anecdotes from their parents or grandparents.'

'Do you think they really believed in them?'

Ms Delauney doesn't answer. She's staring at my art book, which is now lying open. I must have knocked it when I was looking through the papers.

'I'm sorry, I didn't mean to pry, but is that a drawing of a knocker by any chance?' she asks.

'Kind of,' I mutter, although I can't look at her. 'I didn't want to make them look like Disney's Seven Dwarfs or anything . . .'

'What a wonderful drawing,' she says, looking down at her cup of tea, stirring it around as her eyes don't leave the spoon.

'I know my art isn't that good. I just like doing it.'

She carries on stirring her tea. When she finally speaks

it's so quiet it's almost a whisper. 'There are all kinds of artists, Clover. I know your mother was very talented, but I think your picture shows a deep sensitivity and understanding of the stories.' She looks at me. 'I think it's actually, quite special.'

'Really?' I try not to blush again, but something fizzes inside me.

'Clover, my mother was the most amazing storyteller. She had a magnetism, and people were transfixed by her stories, but, when I dabbled in poetry in my university years, I realised that wasn't my talent.'

'So, you tell different types of stories?'

She pauses as if she's thinking about it and then gives a little smile. 'Yes. I suppose I do . . . but the point is that we all have our own path.'

'Do you think there's some truth in these legends, though? Do you think there was something down in the mines, like a ghost or something?'

Ms Delauney glances at me. 'The day my mother died, a trio of bright butterflies hovered around me as I was wailing to the skies.' There's a glow of tears in her eyes. 'I don't think I've ever seen a group of butterflies flutter so close to me and for so long and, whatever anyone says about the coincidence of it, I felt so powerfully that they were drawn to me and that my spirit was somehow being spoken to by my mother.' She pauses. 'I thought she wanted me to carry on seeing all the beauty in the world. So, yes – I think, in a dark mine for all those hours, the miners might have occasionally had the sense of another being protecting them or playing with them in some way.'

'Maybe they were lonely too,' I say. 'Maybe they needed to invent a different world from the one they lived in.'

Ms Delauney flashes me a smile, and she nods.

Chapter Eighteen

Ruby

June 21st, 1851
Dear Ruby,

I was deeply troubled by your last letter.

My brother's insistence on continuing to rely on enslaved people to work his plantation is, indeed, as you suggest, why I moved to Boston.

When you mentioned that Mary had arrived, I was horrified. He had at least promised that he would not 'purchase' any other human beings, although I do appreciate your hope that he will find a way to bring Mary's brother to the plantation.

You ask about the family 'secret'. I was not surprised. I knew that there had been lots of rumblings in the town and so assumed that you had heard something of it. However, I have gone backwards and forwards over this matter and, as I fear it will not help you, I am loathe to be the cause of any rift between you and your family. I will say that it concerns your grandfather and his wishes in his will. I would ask you to appeal to your father's humanity, which existed once, to learn more about it.

Your loving aunt,
Iris

July 5th, 1851
Dear Iris,

I attempted to speak to Papa and Mama last night at dinner and the night before that, but they just shake their heads and refuse to tell me anything about the secret. I will keep trying. I have no doubt they find me quite tiresome, but that is nothing new, so I am becoming quite immune to it.

Thank you for the books you sent. Mr Thistlewood won't teach me what I want to learn. He thinks it is not 'ladylike' for a girl to be learning about politics or mathematics more complex than an infant might understand. So, at least your books allow me to see a little more of the world. In fact, I find myself so immersed in the lives of Jane Eyre or David Copperfield that sometimes I don't hear a sound, which is quite a good thing until Mama scolds me for being late to dinner or for those tedious lessons.

But back to the point of my letter, and please do not be cross for me asking again but nothing seems to have changed, and I am quite at a loss to know what is happening with Mary's brother, Reuben. Papa will not say if he has even made any enquiries, let alone approached that man, Mr Bolt, who is quite hideous by all accounts. Benjamin will be leaving for some adventure soon. University or travel or something. I dread him going and I do not think I can bear it here anyway. Mary has not looked me in the eye since that day outside the church and today when Tildy served us dinner, bringing out course after course of food when her wrists are so thin they look like they might snap, I felt quite sick.

I have turned it around and around in my mind, Aunt, but there is something else I must ask you. I do not mean to sound forceful or improper, but will you consider my coming to live with you? I do not know what I will do if I have to stay here after Benjamin leaves.

Ruby

Chapter Nineteen

Clover

I see Caterina as soon as I turn off the path. It's been four days since I last brought her any food on the day we went to Winchester, and nearly a week since I've spoken to her. She's sitting on one of the rocks, head drooped and hair falling over the left side of her face. 'Did you wash your hair?' I ask, seeing the shiny thick strands of auburn.

'Yes,' Caterina says proudly. 'In cold water from the stream, though.' She scrunches up her face. She looks different today. Not just her hair but her face seems softer somehow.

'I would have wimped out halfway through and had tons of suds all over my head,' I say.

'I'm used to it – it was hideous to brush though. Must have taken me half an hour and I ended up just breaking off loads of knotty bits . . . Anyway, where did you go?' Caterina asks. 'I haven't seen you for days.'

'I tried to see you – did you find the things I left, and the note?'

'Yes,' Caterina says, but I see her swallow. 'Thank

you,' she adds almost breathily, 'but, Clove,' she says, her voice suddenly energetic, 'I've been really, *really* bored. So, you need to tell me everything you've been doing.'

'We went to my grandmother's office, to look at some documents,' I say. 'And I've been helping Ms Delauney with her research.'

Caterina is studying me with a scowl. 'Is that it?' She twists her mouth around, looking unimpressed, which makes me laugh.

'Well, we were trying to find out some stuff in Winchester. At the office,' I say, wondering how to make it interesting. 'It's a really nice place and it's in one of those ancient town houses.'

'You're not making this sound any better.'

'OK,' I say, giggling at the flatness of Caterina's voice, 'well, maybe it doesn't sound it, but it was actually good.'

'So, I'm willing to be open minded about this, Clove,' Caterina says, so seriously that I can't help letting out another little giggle, 'but you have to try really hard to make it even a *little* interesting.'

'Alright,' I say, remembering what Caterina was like when I first met her, how she made me feel inadequate and boring and a bit useless. But Caterina seems friendly now. She's twiddling with something in her hands, but her arms and shoulders seem relaxed. 'We were trying to find out about the person who started the business and where the money came from.'

'Are you serious?! I think my walks to the stream sound more fun.'

'Maybe they are,' I say, remembering how my head pounded from being inside that windowless room.

'I spotted a dead bird yesterday,' Caterina says.

'Oh no . . . Did you bury it?'

'No, I did not!' She peers at me.' Is that what you would have done?'

'Maybe,' I say quietly, blushing. 'I mean, I think it's nicer for the bird. Not just leave it out to be ravaged by a fox or something . . .' I don't tell her that sometimes I'd even recite a short poem or clap my hands together and then open them and my eyes at the same time, trying to imagine that I could send its spirit out into the skies.

'But why is all that office stuff important anyway?' Caterina asks.

'I know it sounds weird, but it's a kind of mystery. We're trying to find out about my great-great-grandfather who started the business. There was kind of a family rift.'

'Isn't that a bit ridiculous? I mean, wasn't that billions of years ago?'

'Oh no,' I say, surprised that I end up laughing again. 'I mean, *recently*. There was a row between my mum and grandparents . . . And it turns out I have a grandmother in Winchester – an uncle and cousins even.'

'Well, of course you have,' Caterina says. 'Doesn't everyone? I mean, I've got about twenty of them.'

'Really? Do you know them all?'

'We all lived in the same village – well, at least, we did until some of them had to move away to get work.' She pauses. 'I didn't have any brothers and sisters, though. Well, I had one, but she died when she was little.' She shrugs, letting her hair fall down over her face so that I can't see her eyes.

'That's awful . . .'

'My mum never really recovered from that.' For a moment, I wonder if I should hug her, but she's scratching something in the ground with a twig, shut off in her own little space, so I end up not doing anything.

'Did you bring your art book?' she says, suddenly looking up. She tries to smile, but there's no light in her eyes.

'Here,' I say, taking out the sketch pad. There's something strange about her today, a sadness or darkness that seems to hover around her. Mum could be like that sometimes and, on those days, I'd stay away, imagining a circle around her that I couldn't go inside, although I hadn't wanted to anyway because, when she was like that, she could be brittle, snapping at the slightest thing.

Caterina slowly turns the pages of the sketch book. 'Where's this?' she asks, as she stares intently at every detail.

'It's the cove, a few miles down the road.'

She carries on studying the drawing. 'It looks nice,' she says. 'You like stones.'

'Yes,' I say.

'Are you one of those people who collects them and carries them around?' she asks.

'Well, I *like* them. But I think you're supposed to leave them on the beach.'

'You're a real goody-goody, aren't you?'

'*No*,' I say, suddenly irritated. 'Look, I get that you're sad, but you don't need to lash out all the time.'

She looks at me, surprised at first, but then giggles. 'So, do you have any with you?' she asks, her voice softer. 'Sorry.'

I dig around my pocket, eventually finding a pebble that I found on the beach with Dad a few days ago. 'There,' I say, handing it over. Caterina silently turns over the stone for a few seconds. When she gives it back, she gently places it into my hand so that I feel the soft pressure of her palm for a little longer than I expect. 'It's funny,' she says. 'I wouldn't have noticed all those little lines on it unless I'd seen them on the drawing. I suppose we must search for the remarkable in things sometimes.' She pauses for a moment, suddenly shy. 'I'm sorry, Clover. I don't know why I snapped at you like that.'

'It's OK,' I say. 'But I don't have to come here.'

'Is that a threat?'

'No. I mean, if you don't want me to be here.'

'Of *course* I want you to come. I suppose it's just been a while since I've been with people who are, well, normal . . . and nice.' Something passes over her face, like a cloud or something and her eyes are so heavy that it makes me shudder. 'I've just spent a lot of time with people who are really cruel.'

'I'm sorry,' I say. 'I get that things are really difficult for you . . .'

'Anyway, Clover,' Caterina says abruptly. 'Do you think you could draw *me*?'

'Alright,' I say, sensing a little flush of pleasure as I take out the pencils and set them out in a line, 'but you'll have to sit still.'

Caterina crouches down on a rock while I draw, trying to get the arch of her eyes right – like a cat, alert and questioning, with that green colour that's almost bewitching. It's difficult, though, and I keep having to change the strokes until eventually it looks something like Caterina, the slightness of her face and slanting eyes and the shock of reddish mousey-brown hair that falls over her face, so that her long eyelashes almost touch her hair.

Caterina starts moving around, striking different poses as if she's a model.

'Stop!' I call out, laughing. But something makes me

add a few lines near her eyes, sharpening the shape of her eyes slightly, the angle of her dark eyebrows.

'Here,' I say, shyly handing over the sketch book.

'I look like a witch,' Caterina eventually says.

'Well, I sometimes exaggerate a bit, you know,' I stutter, 'like cheekbones or the shape of the eyes . . . but I like witches anyway.'

Caterina laughs. 'I like the way you draw.'

'Do you want to keep it?'

'No. He'll see it.' She takes hold of my wrist, gently turning it to see the dial of my watch. 'I need to go,' she gasps, jumping up. 'Thank you,' she adds, glancing at me.

'Caterina,' I say. 'I was trying to make you look . . .' I hesitate, not wanting to annoy her or insult her. 'Sort of like a *fairy*. You know a *mischievous* fairy.'

But Caterina just nods. 'I thought it was a bit like that too . . .'

It's two in the morning. I can't sleep. I can't stop thinking about Caterina and how sad she seemed, so I turn on my side light. I pick up my book from the table next to my bed, trying to be quiet because I can hear Dad awake next door, tapping on his computer.

I look at the postcard I was using as a bookmark. I bought it the day before we went to Lyme Regis, and it has two New Forest ponies in the picture. I don't know why but I suddenly think about Heather at the school. She seemed nice, and she even gave me her address. I twirl the pen around my fingers, wondering if it's a stupid idea because Heather might have forgotten me by now and think it's ridiculous to get a postcard when she hasn't heard from me for weeks. Months, even. But then I remember how friendly she was when she brought out all the jewellery and paintings that last day. And she didn't *have* to give me her address, after all.

I turn over the postcard, eventually managing to write:

Dear Heather, how are you?

Caterina would definitely say that was boring.

We are in Cornwall staying at a place by the sea. It's nice and there's an interesting woman who writes about folklore who I'm helping with research.

This wasn't going much better, but I realise that I don't know Heather, not really anyway. How would I know if she'd think the heath was beautiful, or that the light looked like a painting, which is pretty much all I wanted to say? In the end I scrawl out:

Sorry, that probably doesn't sound very exciting to you, but I like that kind of thing! Anyway, I hope you're enjoying school. I hope you all managed to see Ayesha's puppy. I'm sure he is very cute, and I would love to see a picture.

I copy out Heather's address on the postcard, putting the address of the hostel at the bottom of the postcard, just in case she wants to write back because she was really kind and had a big smile that made her eyes crinkle.

Something makes me think about Caterina and how mean she said people had been. I get my art book out of the bag, flicking through the pages to the portrait of her. I don't know why but I carefully write the date and my name at the foot of the picture, adding a little flourish on the C. Underneath the drawing, I start to write *The Fairy Witch*, but something stops me. *Spriggan Child*, I eventually write in bold, elaborate writing, suddenly wondering whether it might be true.

Chapter Twenty

Clover

The weekend after we visited the office, we arrange to meet Grandma in a restaurant in Winchester. Dad thinks it will be 'easier' to meet somewhere 'neutral'. He thinks it will make me feel like I have 'more control' or whatever line he uses all the time, but my heart is pounding the whole way there.

Dad gets out the pack of cards after he catches me looking at the clock and restaurant door for the millionth time. 'I'm nervous too,' he says quietly, 'if that helps.'

'It doesn't really,' I say, my heart beating so fast I think I might faint, until a tall, slim woman with grey hair and blue eyes walks through the door. She's about seventy but she doesn't seem old exactly. She reminds me of one of those people who seem to gradually *mature*, groomed hair greying as they get a few more lines across their face, but they still speak in the same way as they always did.

When she spots us sitting in a corner table, she walks towards us with a brisk, energetic step. 'Isaac,' she says warmly.

Dad leaps up, but her eyes flicker over towards me. I

know I should feel some sort of emotion, but I don't know this woman at all, and I don't know what to do so, for a few seconds, we stare at each other. Until Grandma smiles and holds out her arms.

I stand up, my legs like jelly, hoping she can't see the little nerve throbbing under my eye, but she just winds her willowy arms around me. It feels strange at first. It's something to do with her straight back and chin that seems slightly raised, and the smell of perfume which reminds me of Mum. But then I hear a little sound, as if she's catching her breath, and, when I hug her properly, she grips me so tight that I can feel her smile on my face.

'Tea, Evelyn?' Dad asks when Grandma finally stops gripping my hand.

'Oh yes, of course,' she says, smoothing her clothes as she sits down.

I'd wondered if Grandma would be like Mum, but when I look at her, I notice a sharpness in her movements which is the opposite of Mum. It's something about the way she places down her bag and takes up her napkin, gently flicking it before placing it on her lap. 'I have been wanting to meet you again for a very long time,' she says, still studying me with that steady gaze. 'You're not really like your mother. Not so much,' she adds, nodding. I wonder if she's a little bit pleased, because if *she'd* been too much like Mum, I think it would have been hard for me too. But then she says, 'You have her eyes, of course, but otherwise you are distinctly *Clover.*' Her smile cracks into a laugh and her eyes twinkle with warmth. 'So, I understand that you are on rather an exciting road trip?'

I nod, not sure what to say.

'And which places have you enjoyed the most?'

'I really like Cornwall.'

'Cornwall is beautiful – slightly craggy, but arresting and rather wild . . .' She purses her lips a little, her eyes narrowing and there's a little nod, almost as if we're sharing a secret. 'Your mother, of course, loved the sea.'

'Dad loves it too,' I say, although I don't know why, but when I glance at him, Dad still has the same calm expression. In some people it might seem distant or unfriendly, but in Dad it's somehow comforting. Like nothing can shock him. Like I could do anything, and he would still be there.

Except for the fact that he *wasn't* always there.

'Yes, well, you always seemed to me to be rather like your father. Curious and observant,' she laughs lightly. 'And *kind*. One of my fondest memories of you is how you cared for a tiny, injured bird that we found in the park, cradling it in your hand for hours, determined to breathe some life back into it.'

I search my brain for any fragment of memory because I want to remember it. I want to have some kind of past that makes sense. But I don't remember the bird.

I suddenly feel sick. Dad touches my hand quickly. 'It's OK,' I say quietly. And something about the feather-like tickle of his finger reminds me of a bird.

'Mum loved birds,' I say.

'Yes,' Grandma says. 'Sometimes I felt like we were as different as can be – antelopes locking horns.' She laughs but the little sound is cut off and her eyes fill with tears. 'But birds were something we shared. Except that she didn't like the swallow. Which was my favourite, of course.' Grandma smiles weakly. 'I knew that she loved the freedom that birds signified, but, for me, the swallow said summers. Moments of light and long days.'

Dad smiles, almost shyly for a moment, a little flicker

in his eyes, his rock-like calm finally shaken.

We are there for two hours. I thought it would be difficult to talk to Grandma but it's actually quite easy. She asks lots of questions but doesn't feel as intense as some people do and she tells me about my uncle and my cousins, who are both boys, and are nine and seven. 'Liam likes photography and is very sweet; Connor every kind of dance – contemporary and ballet and street dance - and he is funny. He is a great mimic,' Grandma says so that I feel a short pang of envy because she knows them so well.

Grandma hugs me tight when she leaves. 'I can't tell you how wonderful it is to have the opportunity to get to know you again,' she says and, even though her eyes seem steady and clear, I hear her voice shake. 'This is for you,' she says, handing me a large envelope.

I watch as she walks to the door, crossing the road, her back tall and straight like a dancer.

I don't open the parcel until we are in the car. When I realise what it is, I let out a little gasp. It's more letters. Pages of letters from Mary and Ruby.

'What is it?' Dad asks with a small frown.

'It's the next part of the story,' I say, my heart beating a little faster.

Chapter Twenty-One

Mary

July, 1851
Dear R,

Everything changed that day at the church. And my story sort of changed too, which is the only way I can explain the next part, because it's a thousand little things, not one word or action but a thread that began to unravel so that what I needed to do eventually became luminous and clear . . .

It's four weeks after the day at the church, when Martha whispers to me, 'Did you really think they'd just go on out and demand that Massa Bolt sells him?'

'I thought they might,' I say.

She tuts. 'You, Mary, are an item of property in their eyes. Nothing more. They do anything at all because it's convenient to them. No other reason. You'd do well to remember that.' She grasps my hand and squeezes it. 'Anyway, at least now your brain decided to get working again. Not like all that nonsense where you were playing dolls with Ruby like you were one of her rich privileged friends.'

'Well, I was never doing that,' I say, 'but Ruby's not so bad.'

Martha shrugs. 'We'll see how she turns out.'

'Don't you ever think about it, though?' I ask. 'Running away.'

'I think about it all the time,' Martha says, studying me with something in her eyes I can't work out, like sadness and anger are all turned around and mixed up together. I see it often. That rage that's always there a little bit, even when she's smiling or singing her heart on out, clear and pure, her arms wrapped tight around Tildy. 'I think about it every second of every minute of every hour, in fact,' she adds, 'though I couldn't leave Momma . . . Her breathing's so bad she couldn't get more than a mile before falling down flat.'

'Would you know how to?' I whisper after a few seconds.

She glances at me, her eyes narrow like small moons. 'I think so,' she says with a little nod.

Things have changed. I sense it each morning in the air and in the grasses that blow in the wind. The spaces between the stars and earth have shifted somehow. Ruby still hovers around the kitchen most days when it's not so hot you might faint. She tries to talk until Tildy tells her that she will get into trouble for not getting things done in time.

'Well, let me help,' she says, but Tildy just lets out that 'uh-uh' sound in the way that she does, shaking her head and her face closed and hard. 'Not going to be making that mistake, Miss Ruby, not even for you,' she adds, which makes Ruby scowl, and then blush some, her face tinged with fire.

Sometimes we still go for walks around the grounds, occasionally stopping in the shadows to cool off from the sun. One day, leaning against the bark of the tree, so hot that we fan ourselves with the large leaves, our eyes itching from the sun and wind, Ruby says, 'What do you do, Mary?' She flushes pink-red when I look at her, confused. 'Apart from all the cleaning and all,' she says, before she adds, 'In the evening, I mean.'

'Play music sometimes,' I say. *'Or tell stories.'*

'And what was your momma like?' she asks.

I haven't talked about Momma in such a long time my heart beats faster and, when I speak, I can tell that my voice is just a whisper. *'She was kind. People say she had a big imagination.'*

'Do you tell stories as well, Mary?' she asks.

'Sometimes.'

'But where do the stories come from if you can't read and if you don't have books?'

I glance at her, trying to work out whether she can mean it, but she's just looking at me, and her forehead, which often looks like a porcelain doll's, creases up.

'I don't really know,' I say. *'But always been stories. Grandmas tell their children, and they tell their children . . .'* Her eyes widen. *'They're not my only stories, though,'* I say, without really meaning to.

'What do you mean?'

'I got my story inside too,' I say. *'I have a story that I tell myself and then I add to it. Like I'm growing something, I suppose.'*

'Like dreams, do you mean?' she asks.

'Yes, well, kinda, but also like that's the real me. My momma taught me. That the outside can't be touched, that it can be like a rock, but that inside I can be flying. Making a different life. And different sorts of memories.'

'I like the sound of that,' she says, looking me straight in the eye until I look away.

Benjamin is usually at school. But when he comes home, he often appears at Ruby's room, standing shyly at the door before he eventually comes in and sits with us. But one time, Ruby's mother calls her down leaving me and Benjamin alone. I try to carry on staring at the book, pretending I'm not aware of the distance between us, that pressure and heat like there's an invisible connection. But he just glances at me awkwardly, and says, almost as if it's a question, 'I could teach you a bit more.' At first, I blush, willing him to stop looking at me with that intensity as I struggle to read the words, but Benjamin just corrects me quietly. 'No, it's a bit of a strange spelling, that one.'

Ruby marches back in after a few minutes. She doesn't seem to notice the strange fizzing in the air. 'Mama just gave me a lecture,' she says, tossing her head. 'She said she doesn't mind if I am friends with you but to be a bit careful about it . . .' And then she says, 'Honestly, it's outrageous.' She shoots a look at Benjamin. 'Doesn't know you're in here, of course. She thinks you're doing schoolwork or something, golden boy.'

Benjamin shifts around, blushing crimson, which he does a lot. I glance at him when I think he can't see me, thinking about Tildy's words a few days earlier. He'd been in the kitchen, too embarrassed to hang around like Ruby. Tildy said she could see that he was heading headlong towards manhood or something. But then she said, suddenly serious, 'I know Benjamin since he was born. Ruby has a tongue on her, but she just frustrated. And I trust Benjamin to behave proper but . . .' She paused for so long I was scared what she'd say. 'Won't be the first of these boys that fallen off a bit. All that growing and pressures from his friends at school . . . You just make sure Ruby there all the time. Or someone else.'

'What do you mean?' I ask.

'She means don't let him touch you,' Martha said in a cold, flat voice, coming in from the yard.

Chapter Twenty-Two

Clover

'What was your grandma like?' Caterina asks. I hadn't seen her for five days. It was too difficult to get out without Dad asking a thousand questions, and the last time I managed to sneak out before breakfast, Caterina didn't turn up.

'She was really nice,' I say.

Caterina seems even more skinny. More so than in my drawing. She'd been thin then with jutting out bones and alert eyes. Not beautiful exactly, but *interesting*. But now she looks ill.

'Did it feel strange to meet her?'

'Yep,' I say. 'I mean, I was very nervous. But she was sort of easy to be with.' I glance at Caterina. There's a small tremor in her face, which just seems to get worse, until her whole face is quivering. '*You* have this,' I say, handing her my jacket, 'I'm not cold.'

'No, I can't!' She shakes her head so vigorously I take it back.

'Well, I'm hungry, anyway,' I say, emptying out my bag, and laying out some apples and grapes and the sandwiches I made.

I eat slowly, waiting for Caterina to finish her sandwich before I take too many bites. 'I've had enough,' I say, hoping she'll eat the rest of the picnic. 'Caterina . . . are you OK? I mean, you seem thin and ill. And that man . . .'

She gives me such a ferocious look that I flinch. 'He's fine. I'm fine,' she says.

'But you're so hungry. You seem ill . . .I can help you. I can tell my dad. Or the police or something.'

'If you tell anyone, we'll have to leave and then that will be even worse because I will disappear and maybe starve.'

I stare at her, wondering what to say. And what if she's right? I fiddle around with some twigs on the ground, trying to think of an idea, but, if Caterina doesn't see me again, how can I help her?

'Sorry,' Caterina says after a few minutes of silence. 'And thank you for the food.' She smiles at me although it doesn't seem like a real smile somehow. 'Anyway, what does "nice" mean?' asks Caterina, when she's finished a second sandwich. 'With your grandma?'

'Kind, I suppose,' I say. 'And sort of unflappable. But she laughs a lot . . . and she seems to like my dad.'

'So?'

'Well, my parents broke up.'

'Maybe she sympathises with him,' Caterina suggests, which surprises me for a second. 'She was sort of rejected by your mum too.'

'Dad left *us*,' I say. But then I remember the letter Dad gave me a few weeks ago, which is still at the bottom of the box because I can't face reading it.

Caterina just plays around with some loose bark on the damp ground. 'Do you think your grandma is like your mother at all?'

'Not really,' I say.

'Is that a good or bad thing, do you think?'

For a moment I wonder what to say, but Caterina is just waiting, not disapproving or frowning.

'I suppose in a way, it's a *good* thing,' I say eventually. 'I really loved my mum . . . but I'm not sure if I would want *another* of her exactly.' I stop, trying to control the tremor in my voice. 'I mean, I wish she was here now. I wish that every single day . . .'

'But some things you'd prefer to have been different?'

'Not *her*, exactly. But how we lived. You know, on our own all the time.'

'My mum gave me away,' Caterina says. 'My uncle said it was because they were poor and was nothing to do with her feelings about me, but I don't think that can be true, do you?'

I don't know what to say but Caterina's still looking at me. 'Maybe they *were* poor. Maybe she thought it would give you some kind of opportunity.'

'I don't think so, my mother could get angry about the smallest thing,' she says, taking a deep breath, 'but, at night-time, when she didn't have to work, she told me stories. The darker the better, her hands jerking and stretching into shapes on the wall . . . Most of the time they were scary,' Caterina says, 'And really weird. You know, axemen and stuff. But I still liked them.'

'Why?'

'Because when I watched her eyes, they would fizz with electricity. And at least, when she was telling the stories, she was just thinking about me. And it was only us two. Her and me . . .' There's a flash of something in her eyes that I can't work out. Rage and sadness. I don't know why but, for a few seconds, she reminds me of a little girl, until she straightens up and fixes her eyes on me. 'But one March afternoon, she walked out. And I sat there, watching her, her back tall and straight as she disappeared through trees. I remember thinking that the thick frost looked like icing sugar. Like it was beautiful and magical.' She blinks. 'And then I realised that she was actually leaving for good.' She glances at me. 'And do you know the worst thing? She didn't look back. Not once. She just kept walking through those trees like she could somehow become part of the forest.'

'Do you miss her?'

Caterina shrugs. 'Sometimes something reminds me of her. Random stuff. I hear a bird, or smell something, like flowers or a particular type of soap and think of her.' She twists her thumbs. 'Even something about the way someone moves their hands makes me think of my mum sometimes.'

'I know what you mean,' I say. 'My grandma's fingers were the only things that reminded me of Mum – she has really thin fingers and these bony knuckles and Mum's hands were a bit like that . . .' My voice trails off. I don't know if I can say it.

'What's wrong?' Caterina asks quietly.

'I think . . .' I stop, because I don't know if I can tell her what I'm feeling even though sometimes it keeps me awake at night.

'Whatever you say, I promise I won't think it's bad.'

I look at her, wondering if she's telling the truth but she's just looking at me, her eyes wide and unblinking.

'I think I'm angry with my mum,' I say eventually. 'I mean, not just with the situation or with my dad and the fact he left us, but with *her*.'

I glance at Caterina, but her expression doesn't change.

She's just listening, fiddling around with the bark and the twigs in the earth.

'That's OK,' she says after a few seconds. 'I'm angry with mine too. I'm angry that she gave me up.'

'But I *hate* feeling like this,' I say softly. 'I mean, sometimes I feel like I'm letting her down – and that feels terrible because she's dead.' Caterina looks right at me. She seems almost frozen, her hands placed on her knees. 'But all these things. All these people that I'm getting to know . . . everything is different from what I thought. And now I can't even ask her.' I turn away slightly, staring at something on the ground. It's too difficult to tell her when she has that that intense expression on her face. 'Sometimes I try not to think about it too much, but then something reminds me of her, and I feel this pain in my stomach, or chest, and it makes me feel like screaming . . . and then I remember anyway.'

'Remember what?'

'That I can't ever talk to her again. Not just now, but not *ever*. And sometimes that's too difficult to take in.' I swallow. 'Sometimes I feel like I'm drowning . . .'

I look at Caterina but she's motionless, the breeze gently blowing her hair over her eyes in a rhythmic, mesmerising motion.

She doesn't say anything but moves towards me, sitting down on the ground next to me. And then she puts her arm around me.

For a few seconds, all I can feel is the movement in the cool air, tickling my hair, and Caterina's hand on my arm. I start to cry, the tears falling until I'm panting with short loud breaths, but Caterina just rests her head on my shoulder.

'I used to think I knew everything about my mum,'

I say when I can speak. 'I thought we had this amazing bond. I mean, if we didn't, then nothing would be worth it, would it? I mean, all that time, it was just me and her. And I didn't have my dad or my grandma.'

'I think you *did* have an amazing bond.'

'There was a day in the hospital just after Mum collapsed. She was so ill that she couldn't even speak but she gave me this *look*. Even then, when she was so ill, and her lips were purple, I thought I knew what it meant, so I climbed on the bed and put my arms around her. She was so fragile, you know, like an injured bird, her chest rising and falling. And I said, 'I love you so much too, Mum,' and she just nodded . . . I thought she was telling me that she loved me, that that was what her eyes were saying. But since then, I wonder whether I was wrong . . .'

'Clover, your mum really loved you.' She says it so simply that I look at her. 'She really loved you,' she says again staring right at me until I nod.

It's nearly midnight when I take out the box. I slowly open Dad's letter, my hands shaking.

So yesterday I left. And you wouldn't even look at me, my darling Clover . . .

Suddenly everything comes rushing at me – the smell, even the taste, of the room, and Dad walking towards the door. It slammed behind him, and the hallway shelves rattled and there was an echo of glass against china, like a delicate, fragile chain of sound.

So yesterday I left. And you wouldn't even look at me, my darling Clover, you just stared at your doll, twisting its arms as if you wanted to break them off. I touched your hand. It felt so soft, almost like a rag doll. Maybe it is better for you that I leave, and you don't hear all our terrible arguments. But I hope you know how much I love you. I hope you'll remember that, and the stories I used to tell you and the way we'd sometimes laugh.

But, staring at the empty walls, I can't understand how it happened. I should have been able to make it better, but I couldn't.

And now I feel like the two people I love most in the world are gone and I would do anything to be back there – to just stand silently, listening to the gentle movement of the Noah's ark clock on the wall, as I stare at you, sleeping in your bed as you fidget a little, clinging to your doll Jemima.

I read it twice and then I place the pages under my pillow, wanting to keep hold of those words, as if whispered to me again: *my darling Clover.*

Chapter Twenty-Three

Ruby

July 14th, 1851
Dear Aunt Iris,

I am writing this late at night. The light from the lamp is weak and I must squint to see the letters, but I was silly enough to think that writing to you might stamp out some of my frustration because, so far, Aunt, nothing has changed here. There is still no news of Reuben. Papa refuses to listen and, after dinner tonight, he looked at me as if I were just a nuisance and marched on into his study, closing the door. I hoped Mama might support me for once, but she gave me a pitying look and went to her room. So, it is all quite dreadful.

There is another thing that I wanted to tell you, although with all your important meetings it will probably sound too silly to be bothered with, but I can't stop it from going round and round my head until I feel I will go quite mad with it all. Everything has been horrid since that day at the church. Mary does not look at me the same. I can tell that she is cross or sad that nothing has been done about Reuben, which I can understand, and to be truthful, I don't feel like I can look at her the same either. But today she at least agreed to come to my room, and we lay on the floor, turning the pages of the atlas. It sounds childish, I know, especially when you have such important work to do, but we look at the maps and rivers and mountains and think about where we'd like to go. Sometimes Mary will imagine going to enormous waterfalls where the water must sound like thunder, and to the Amazon jungle where they have enormous butterflies and strange insects that she thinks her brother would like. I imagine going to Japan because it sounds beautiful and exotic, don't you think? But today Mary shook her head when I mentioned the game and instead, I saw her finger tracing the path of the River Mississippi.

Aunt, I knew that she was thinking about her brother, and I had a quite alarming thought that made my blood run cold that she would try to find him herself. But then she forced a smile, although I could tell that she was still sad.

'I'm sorry it's so unfair,' I said. 'When I'm sixteen or eighteen or whatever I have to be,' I told her, 'I'm going to leave here and live with my aunt in the North.'

I quite blush now with thinking about what a foolish thing it was to say, but all she said was, 'I wish I could go there too.'

I mean it though, Aunt, even if it won't help Mary or Tildy much. So please let me come and live with you in Boston. Even if I can't do anything clever and impressive like your lawyer friends or those people that give great speeches, I promise I will try to learn to be useful.

Your loving niece,
Ruby

Chapter Twenty-Four

Mary

August, 1851
Dear R,

It's late when I walk across the yard that afternoon. The sun is getting lower and is starting to settle behind the barn roof. I glance at the stables, listening for the sound of the horses braying, or Abe's voice, because he likes to talk to them, brushing and brushing their manes as he murmurs their names. But this time I see Benjamin coming out of the stables. He must have been for a ride, his boots still on as he strides across the yard.

He doesn't see me at first, so I move farther away, finding a tree to hover beneath, hoping the dark shadows from its long, twisting branches will keep me hidden. I see a frown criss-crossing between his eyes, but I stay completely still and stare up at the bits of blue left in the sky between the leaves which are spread over above me like a decorated parasol.

'Mary,' he says, suddenly seeing me. His voice croaks and sounds strange.

'You surprised to see me Benjamin?' I say, staying still

under the branches as he comes towards me. 'And you never asked your father.'

Benjamin doesn't say a thing. He just bites the corner of his lip, and I notice his fingers making little twisting movements until he makes them into fists, stretching them out again in quick jerks.

'I know you feel bad,' I eventually say, although I can't keep the edge of bitterness out of my voice. 'But I trusted you.'

'Mary.' He's now standing less than a metre away. We are both hidden by the branches of the tree, and he's so close to me that I can feel my heart beating, a rapid rhythm, except it's all mixed in with a sick feeling, because I know that something isn't right about this. And that love and hate are all so mixed together that I don't know how to prise them apart.

Benjamin studies me, gently shaking his head. He touches my hand, and something shoots straight through my palm and fingers so I almost jolt. I don't know why it feels like this. Ruby touches me sometimes, gently nudging me when we look at the atlas, or when she's talking about how she wants to see things – travel down the Amazon, looking for sloth bears in the trees, or brightly coloured birds with painted wings, like parrots or parakeets. But this makes me edge away, remember Martha's words – 'Don't let him touch you' – even though I'm almost sure Benjamin won't hurt me.

Benjamin glances at me, his eyes making my heart race again, and he gently takes my hand. His fingers grip around my fingers in a tight circle and I think I can feel his pulse gently throbbing. 'Shall we go for a walk, Mary?' he asks.

This time I nod, letting him tug me along towards the little sandy trail at the back of the plantation. We walk behind the sheds and cabins and that patch of grass and mud where the goats are kept until we reach a drooping, twisty old tree and a weathered stump, which looks like it's almost floating above the dust and gravel.

'What is it then?' I ask, suddenly impatient, wanting to stop this thud and flutter of my heart which is sending my head into a mass of questions.

'Mary,' he says softly, unable to look me in the eye, 'I spoke to my father. I told him what I heard about Mr Bolt.'

'What have you heard?' I ask, a slow sickness creeping up towards the back of my neck and creating all these prickles.

Benjamin swallows. 'That he beats his workers until they pass out sometimes.' He looks at his hands. 'He doesn't respect the women either.' He says through gritted teeth his face reddening.

'I reckon I know that already,' I say.

He looks at me. 'What do you mean?'

'My momma never told me, but I thought maybe Massa Bolt was my father. Him or one of those overseers.' I swallow. 'Momma hated them but there wasn't much she could do. And I probably wasn't the only one.'

Benjamin's mouth is open still. 'He treated his children like that? Worked them from dawn to dusk.'

'Beat them too . . .but we were all just belongings to him. And, even if it's true, I wasn't his child. Not properly. Momma and Pete were the ones who told me stories and who tried to teach me who I really am.' Benjamin's eyes stay fixed on the ground. 'Have you heard anything else about Massa Bolt,' I ask, wondering why Benjamin still can't look at me.

'Last week I heard that he sent a patteroller out after someone who escaped. Apparently, he strung him up and left him hanging for days.'

'Who was it?' I gasp, thinking of Michael or Samuel – or old Jacob with his fiddle that he played so that his fingers and knees moved with the rhythm.

'I don't know,' he says, grasping hold of a stick and drawing a strange pattern in the dirt. 'Mary,' he says quietly, 'we found out two days ago that Mr Bolt already sold Reuben. And he refuses to say where . . .'

For a few seconds, I can't breathe.

'I'll ask my father again. Maybe he can find something else out,' Benjamin says. 'We can still try.'

I know it's not his fault, but I still look up and fix my eyes on him. 'Just go,' I say sharply, seeing a flash of pain flit across his eyes, before he trudges away.

I hunch over, pressing my face into my skirts and sob. I don't know how long I'm there for but, when I finally stop, the sun has started spreading its colours further across the horizon, bands of yellow and pink stretching across the sky. I rub my eyes with my skirt. I have to go back and help Tildy. But, when I pass the old tree, I see him, leaning against the bark, watching me.

That night, I dream of Reuben, as though he has somehow dissolved into the sky, floating alongside the stars and moon. And in the morning, I pass the old oak tree at the edge of the yard. I see the piece of paper immediately, folded and fastened in place with the stem of a leaf.

We finally found out. Papa told me when he got home. He's in Kentucky.

I can't dance when Abraham plays his fiddle that evening, however much he winks at me, and I don't smile when Rachel puts her hand in mine. And just before I go to bed, I whisper, 'Martha, I need to get away from here.'

Her worn, tired eyes cloud over for a few moments, but then she nods.

Chapter Twenty-Five

Clover

We go back to Winchester the week after we met Grandma. It's Dad's idea.

'Do you think they will be able to trace any of the other letters?' I ask when we're back at the office.

'I hope so,' Dad says, pouring himself a cup of coffee from the cafetière.

'We still don't know what happened,' I say. 'I mean, did Ruby ever leave? And did Mary escape?'

'Sorry,' Priya says, bustling in, 'I had to phone your grandma. They found some documents in the other office,' she says, 'so, we have to get them copied and sent over, which might take a while, I'm afraid.'

'That's fine. There's no particular rush,' Dad says diplomatically, glancing at me. 'We'll go out for a bit of a breather and some lunch,' he says, picking up his jacket.

I didn't see it before but there's a black and white photograph on the wall by the reception desk. I look at it more closely. It's dated in 1863 and shows a line of people queuing along the street, a man in a suit opening the doors. 'Was the shop always successful?' I ask.

'That was when they opened the main shop in London. The first was much smaller, but it did quite well, although at times it was harder, of course,' Priya says.

'What do you mean?' I ask.

'They were restricted on what they were willing to sell.'

'How do you mean?' Dad asks.

'They wouldn't sell American cotton,' Priya says. 'They refused.'

'Why?' Dad asks.

'Because it was picked by people who were enslaved,' I say.

It's too early to meet Grandma so we go to the cathedral. Afterwards, we sit on the grass while a brass band belts out songs from musicals.

After twenty minutes, I glance up and spot Grandma in the distance, walking briskly towards us. 'Ice creams already!' she says with mock disapproval when she reaches us as she studies the strawberry and salted caramel deliciousness in our hands.

'Would you like one?' Dad asks, gesturing towards the ice cream van.

'Well, I think I will,' Grandma says, eyes twinkling. She lays down her coat on the grass, sitting next to me. 'And what have you been up to since I last saw you, Clover?' she asks.

'Not that much really,' I say, suddenly wondering what's left to say because I can't talk about Caterina. 'I walk a lot and sometimes I help Ms Delauney with her research . . .'

'The anthropologist you mentioned before?' she asks. 'She seems to be rather an interesting woman.'

'She is,' I say. 'And she's really nice too.'

'You seem to have found something of a kindred spirit

there,' she says. 'I always enjoyed research in my younger years. I even thought of becoming a journalist.'

'Really? Why didn't you?' I ask.

'Oh, things were different then. And I think my parents were keen for me to take the reins at *Iris*. They couldn't understand the idea of chasing what they considered a pipe dream when they had a rewarding business that could provide me with a solid future . . .' she glances at me. 'Oh, don't you worry, Clover. I enjoyed it too and it has given me a great deal to indulge my interests over the years. Including these letters of course . . .' She smiles at me. 'Mary's story is really quite remarkable . . . I just wish we knew it all. There are too many gaps to understand exactly what happened. Unfortunately, sometimes people don't value things enough at the time, and only later realise why they are so important. When it's too late.'

'Do you think there are any other letters?' I ask. 'Apart from the ones you found, I mean.'

'When we first investigated the origins of the business, we tried a lot of different possible locations,' Grandma says. 'We contacted a museum in Boston that was founded by Iris Finch, Benjamin's aunt, and also the Finch plantation. The current owners of the Finch plantation seem to be reluctant to help and the museum in Boston was neglected for years so that the archives fell into considerable disarray. But they have now gained some more funding and are determined to make it a success.'

'Did they find anything, though?' I ask, hoping I don't sound too desperate. I'd read the letters so many times I felt like I knew Mary and Ruby. And it wasn't even just that. I also needed to know whether Mum was right, which was even more confusing. I didn't want Benjamin to have used the profits of slavery. But I didn't want Mum to have cut off Grandma and the rest of her family for no reason either. I wanted there to be a point, at least.

'They have a new curator which is why they are sending things to us in dribs and drabs.' She shakes her head a little. 'But they are confused about Mary's letters too. Or who they were addressed to.'

'Couldn't they be a diary?' I ask. 'They seem so personal. And immediate. Like you could be standing there feeling those things at that time.'

'I've thought that too. But Mary couldn't read at first and, of course, enslaved people weren't allowed to write, so I think they must have been written later . . . which means that we are left with the rather impossible task of trying to fit all the pieces together.'

'Like a patchwork quilt,' I say.

Grandma glances at me sharply, like she is going to ask a question, but Dad comes back with her ice cream.

He sits down beside us on the grass, stretching out his legs.

'Anyway, Clover,' Grandma says, 'how is Cornwall now that spring is nearly here?'

'I really like it,' I say.

'Do you think you'll stay much longer?' Grandma asks, glancing at Dad as she tips the ice cream so that the creamy swirl doesn't fall off.

'A bit,' Dad says, 'although I'm not sure my business can stand much more disruption, and the hostel is starting to get busier.'

'And what do you think, Clover?' Grandma asks gently.

There's a little stab of panic in my chest. I don't want to leave Ms Delauney. And I like the hostel. It feels safe and it's nice being by the sea and hearing the sounds of birds on the heath. **And what about Caterina?**

I study a nearby pigeon attacking the remnants of an ice cream cone a few metres away. 'I like being in Cornwall,' I say. 'And I like Ms Delauney.' Grandma looks at me with a small smile as she nods encouragingly every few seconds, but Dad has a strange expression on his face. 'What is it?' I ask. 'I thought you could do your work online or something.'

'I'm managing to keep it afloat, but there's a limit on how much time I can spend away. I need to meet my clients sometimes and to also find ways of attracting new clients.' He looks at me. 'What do you think about finding somewhere to live, Clovie? I mean, a proper house, but not like that box I lived in before. I was thinking we could live somewhere like Dorset. It's by the sea and not far from here.'

'Would I have to go to school again?' My heart's beating fast and there's a sense of sickness that rises in my throat.

'This time might be better,' Dad says. 'You were dealing with a lot then and there are a lot of good things about school – friends and opportunities that you can't get from worksheets in a hostel dining room, like real science equipment and drama and art studios. . .'

'I thought you said I would get a say this time?'

'I *promise* you'll get a say.' Dad fixes his eyes on me, and I notice those tiny lines around his pupils, which are a strange mixture of sea-green and blue.

I look down, trying to make a chain with daisies while I try to work it all out, focusing on the spindly stems. There's a tiny flutter of excitement in my stomach. Heather was nice. Chioma could always make me laugh with her energy and funny impersonations. And Ayesha showed me pictures of her new puppy, and said I could go around to her house if I liked. And I can remember wanting to say yes.

I hold the daisy chain out. Six daisies. Not quite enough for a chain. There were tons of daisies at the house in Scotland – they grew all around the long grass near the croft. And buttercups . . .

I look back up at Dad and Grandma, seeing their small, fixed smiles as they wait for me to answer. 'Yes, Dad,' I say, although my voice sounds slightly hoarse and strange.

'What's that mean?' asks Dad, with a little laugh. 'Yes, good, or, yes, acknowledgement . . . ?'

'It means that I think I might like it,' I say. But then I think about Caterina and how thin and ill and scared she seems. 'But not yet,' I add.

It's nearly nine when we get back to the hostel. Dad stops in the hostel lobby, talking to one of the cyclists who arrived last night. I go into the living area to find Ms Delauney doing crosswords at the table. 'Did you have a good time?' she asks, placing down her reading glasses.

'Yes,' I say. 'We met up with my grandma again.'

'Clover,' Ms Delauney says quietly, 'a girl came here this afternoon. She wanted to speak to you. I tried to persuade her to stay but she ran off again.' She swallows, looking at me. 'She looked in a bit of a state, I'm afraid. Her name was . . . what was it? Catriona, perhaps?'

My heart stops. I think my breathing stops too. 'Caterina,' I say. Something terrible must have happened. There's no way she'd risk coming here, being seen by people, otherwise.

I feel sick. I shouldn't have listened when she kept saying that it would make things worse. I should have told someone. Dad or Ms Delauney. I should have trusted them to do the right thing.

And now, if anything happens to Caterina it's my fault.

Chapter Twenty-Six

Ruby

September 18th, 1851
Dear Iris,

Benjamin says that any complaints I make will sound petty and so I shouldn't take up your time, but I feel like I will run mad if I don't share this with someone.

Yesterday evening, with the moon full in the sky, I was so restless that I had to find anything I could to distract me. Benjamin was out at one of those truly awful social gatherings, which he detests so much that, afterwards, I feel like I can see bits of rage sparking off him. And Mama seems more distant than usual and spends way too much of the day rocking in that chair on the veranda, which makes me so sad and angry that I want to scream. Anyway, and I hope you won't think too badly of me, but today I went into Papa's study. He is away on business again and I thought I might be able to find out something about the 'secret' that no one will tell me. Anyway, I did find something out, although I can't tell exactly what it means. In a drawer at the back of the bureau was a letter or contract which goes on and on about 'Grandpapa's intentions' and something about a 'promise to free all those who are enslaved.' As far as I can tell from the letter, Grandpa wanted everyone to be free, but the last time I counted, there are still thirty-two people here. Trapped, sleeping in cramped cabins and not being paid a cent to work twelve hours each day.

Aunt, as much as I don't want Papa to despise me, you must tell me now because, unless everything changes soon, I think something might explode.

Ruby

Chapter Twenty-Seven

Mary

September, 1851
Dear R,

Martha is lying in the bed next to me. She curls up into my back and whispers, 'Don't want Momma to hear. She would say it's too dangerous, but you know Samuel's nephew at the plantation with Massa Stokes, over towards Kittysville?'

'Yep.' We sometimes see him at church.

'Well, Samuel's nephew escaped a few weeks back. Not been found by any paddyroller or anything and the massa serious mad and think he probably got away now.'

'To the North?'

'No, need to go farther than that these days. Need to go all the way up. To Canada at least,' she whispers. 'Since that Fugitive Slave Bill, those paddyrolls can just waltz right in there and steal you back, even if you free . . .' A little shot of fear runs through me, remembering Rachel's leg. 'So, apparently, there's a conductor, pretends to be just visiting, doing jobs for the neighbouring plantation.'

'Conductor?'

'It's the Underground Railroad. Don't you know anything

Mary girl?! It's the system of routes that they take you on. Sometimes have to stop at different houses for a night or two.'

'There are people who would risk that?'

'Yes,' Martha says, 'people who used to be enslaved or those who live free in the North. They know what a terrible thing is this kind of life.'

'But what about the safehouses? Isn't it dangerous for people to hide runaways?'

'Course it's dangerous . . . but not everyone short of morals. Some folk actually think about things and don't just blindly go along with evil, and anyway, these conductors been going on these routes before. They know where to go, and there are signs – special patterns on a patchwork quilt. Tell you whether it's safe to go there or not . . .'

'How do you know what they mean, though?'

'You have to learn different patterns, symbols . . . like one looks like a square window, with planks of woods going around it in two layers. It means a log cabin – a safehouse.' She pauses. 'I reckon you won't need them. I reckon you'll go on a boat.'

'But I gotta go find Reuben!'

'Quiet, Mary,' Martha whispers. 'Don't go waking everyone . . . Do you know how far it is to walk to the North?' she says. 'And that's just the start of it. Still vulnerable to being stolen back. No, you have to go by boat.'

I breathe, in and out, trying to calm myself so that I don't go shouting again for everyone to hear. 'Did you tell anyone about me? Did you ask them if they could take me?'

'No, wasn't completely sure you wanted to go that much . . .'

'What would you do, Martha?' I whisper, even though my mind's pretty much made up.

When she speaks, it's in a muffled voice, like she's trying not to cry. 'Mary, this ain't freedom here, just because Miss Ruby and Master Benjamin take a shine to you . . . You smart. You can read and write . . .' I swallow, wondering how she knows that. 'You got a chance.' For a few seconds she's silent, and I wonder if she's sleeping, but then she says in a voice that is hoarse and dry, 'I would just love to know what it would feel to be free. To walk barefoot on a square of grass that I could call mine, and no one telling me to do nothing.'

Every day, just before supper, Martha and I go to the shade of the old oak tree, and she draws the quilt symbols in the dust as small insects run over our feet and tickle our toes.

By the third day, I know them all. The 'north star', the sign that tells you that patterollers are in the area, the 'drunkard's path' and the 'monkey wrench', which say that you need to gather tools to fend for yourself on the journey . . . That one always makes me shudder though – having to build your own shelters out in the open and walk the miles and miles north to reach the river when those patterollers hot on your heels the whole time, their hounds sniffing around for a scent, seems terrifying. And impossible.

Just before we go to sleep that night, Martha turns to me as the moon grows fuller and brighter. 'I envy you,' she whispers.

'Ruby,' I say a few days later, 'can we look at your atlas?'

She glances at me, narrowing her eyes, but still pulls down the battered atlas from the shelf. 'You wanna play the game?' she asks.

I shake my head.

'You never play it properly anyway,' she says, smiling. 'The people in your travels are circling in the sky and diving under the sea.'

'Ruby, where the Ohio River again?' I ask.

'There,' she says, pointing to the blue line twisting and turning across the page. 'And that's Kentucky.'

I follow my finger along the line, trying to imprint the shapes and names, hoping it might help.

'Why do you want to know?' Ruby asks, suspicion returning to her voice.

I try to fix my eyes right to the page. 'Just wondering where my brother Reuben living,' I say, freezing up, but when I glance sideways, I see tears in her eyes. And then I hear the soft shuffle of shoes and see Benjamin, standing still in the doorway.

'I better go and help Tildy,' I say, but he doesn't move out of the way, and so I have to brush past him, touching his hand, a surge of excitement rushing up and down my arm.

When I turn around, Ruby seems transfixed, her eagle eyes searching Benjamin's face and then mine.

'Mary,' I hear Ruby say as I walk quietly down the stairs. To the kitchen. To Tildy, whose eyes penetrate my skin.

Chapter Twenty-Eight

Clover

It had always looked like just a jumble of stones and now even the scraps of fabric are gone from the window. There are no beds or even a cooker, although there's ash inside a ring of stones which might once have been a fire. I wonder how Caterina managed to live here for so long.

'What do you know about this girl?' Ms Delauney asks.

'Not much,' I say. 'Her mum left them.'

'And the man?'

'I don't think he was her father . . .' I try to picture his face, only remembering that it looked rough and fierce. 'But she said that he was OK. That he worried about her.' I swallow, feeling sick. 'I believed her,' I say, 'and she was terrified that I would tell anyone. She said it might make things worse . . .' I feel hot and my hands are sweating. 'What if I was wrong? What if she just told me that because she was scared of him??' Ms Delauney puts an arm around me and squeezes me and, for a second, I rest my head on her shoulder.

'Everything will be alright,' she says, making shushing

sounds. 'She came to the hostel. She could have got away if she needed to.'

I manage a tiny nod of my head wondering if she's right. Caterina found it easy enough to come out and see me and talk to me lots of times, after all. And she went all the way to the hostel by herself. She could have escaped if she needed to. So she must have stayed with him for a reason.

I walk towards the window where I sometimes saw her wave at me, wondering what it felt like sleeping in that place. 'You know, it sounds ridiculous now but when she turned up at the hostel, wild and hair flowing, I thought about the spriggans and the knockers,' Ms Delauney says. 'Like she was this strange, mythical creature . . . but this place is terrible – there's absolutely no romance to somewhere so cold and damp and awful.'

A bitter taste works its way up to my throat and mouth. 'Who do you think she is?' I ask, all the pieces of the puzzle slowly fitting together so that I can only think of one, terrible explanation. But I don't want to say it. 'I mean, why do you think she was living here?'

'I don't know,' Ms Delauney says. 'There are certainly stories in the papers . . .' She pauses.

And then I remember: 'She said they were hiding from someone.'

'Clover,' Ms Delauney says, lightly touching my arm. 'You know that we have to go to the police now? I know you thought you were helping Caterina by keeping quiet, but we must tell someone else now.'

The one mile walk along the coastal path back from the police station takes half an hour, as we trudge slowly along the narrow track one behind the other, trying to work out what happened to Caterina.

'They could have been dangerous,' says Dad, 'and you should have told me.'

'I'm really sorry,' I say, 'but Caterina was terrified about *anyone* finding out about them being there. Every time I said we should tell someone she got angry and told me that I couldn't. I was worried that I might make matters worse.'

'I know,' Dad says, 'but it was way too much for a child – or even an adult – to handle alone.'

'I'm sorry,' I say again. I feel sick still. I can't stop thinking about Caterina and wondering what made her leave. And where she is now.

Dad hugs me, quickly, like he's worried I'll throw him off. 'Everything will be OK,' he says. 'Everything is going to be alright,' he mutters again until I eventually believe him.

It's six o'clock when we get back. 'You hungry?' asks Dad.

'I think I'll just go to bed, read a book or something.'

'Alright,' Dad says. 'Let me know later if you want to eat something. Or just to talk . . . I didn't say it before, Clover, but the sketch of Caterina you showed to the police was really good. You are very talented.'

I don't answer. It seems irrelevant now anyway.

'Clover!' Mr Jakes waves me over to the reception desk. 'There's some post for you.'

I study the small pile, sensing a flutter of excitement when I spot a small envelope that looks like a card. When I turn it over, I see Heather's address written in big round writing on the back. There's also a thick rectangular package in brown paper from Winchester.

I don't open anything until I'm in my room. Heather sends a photo of Ayesha smiling with her puppy and tells me about her school play, which she says was not very good but 'sort of fun'. I read it twice, almost wishing I was still at the school so that I could be in the play and go with Heather and Ayesha to take her puppy for a walk.

The parcel's from Grandma. A stack of papers and an envelope on top with a few lines in black ink.

> *My dear Clover, I have thought of you so often over the years. I can't tell you how happy I am to get to know you again. Much love, Grandma xx*

The envelope contains two photographs. Both are of Mum, although she's only five or six, staring forward with her chin raised a fraction. Her eyes were the same, deep blue and piercing, although in the photo she has a small smile as she holds up a fishing net and bucket. The other is of her graduation, Mum standing tall and proud in her hat and gown. I search the people in the background, my eyes flitting across the faces laughing in the sun until I find a tall man with eyes the colour of the sea – Dad.

At the top of the stack of papers is a note, written by Grandma, although the words are odd and formal.

> *It was so wonderful to see you yesterday and I did not want to fill our lovely afternoon with too many details or facts, so I thought I would jot them down here. You already know something of Mary who, to my deep shame, was enslaved on the Finch plantation. You already know that a fire destroyed many papers relating to the foundation of Iris. However, when we were first investigating the history of the company, we found some of Mary's letters – or diary – together with a few other items, in the museum that Iris*

> *Finch set up in Boston which was dedicated, in part, to the work of some of the abolitionists and the Underground Railroad. These included the correspondence from Benjamin's sister, Ruby, and her aunt Iris, although, as I told you, it was a little chaotic before the current, very enthusiastic, curator took over. They are only now recognising the potential significance of some of the items. Frustratingly, there are still quite a lot of missing pieces to what seems to be an elaborate puzzle, including the rather troubling fact that we cannot work out exactly who Mary's letters were sent to or when they were even written, which must have been later than the dates on them. I can only assume they must be some kind of account, told later. As if she was telling her story. In her words.*

I re-read the last few sentences, thinking about the letters and the fact that Mary wrote them like they were happening then, at that moment like they were diary entries but written for someone else. So maybe Grandma's right. But who were the letters for? Could R be Reuben . . . ? I turn back to the letter.

> *The museum told us that, from what they can tell, there was also once a piece of fabric in the archive, possibly part of a quilt. The curator says that copies of some of the letters were sent to someone a few years ago . . .*

Mum . . .

> *They wonder if the quilt was also sent at that time. The curator thinks it might be a clue to what happened, but it is still missing. I sincerely hope that we will recover some of this wonderful history although I fear that we may have to be patient.*

The quilt. A shiver runs through me. It must have been Mum who tried to get hold of the quilt, but why didn't she tell Grandma? And what else did she discover?

> *In the meantime, I leave you with the first of two small batches of letters that the museum has recently traced. The second batch is still being copied but I will send them to you as soon as I can. I think you will find them rather interesting.*

'Clover!' It's Dad, calling from the bottom of the stairs. 'Are you alright?'

'Yes. Just reading.'

I flick through the pages. There are a few letters from Ruby, one from Iris and another letter, or diary entry, from Mary. But when I look at Ruby's letter again, the words of her first line make me shudder. *Dear Aunt Iris, Something terrible has happened . . .*

I go down to the dining room, two steps at a time. Dad has set out toast and dips and fruit in the middle of the table. 'What is it?' he asks, frowning.

I sit down at the table putting Ruby's letter down on the table in front of him.

Chapter Twenty-Nine

Ruby

September 30th, 1851
Dear Aunt Iris,

Something terrible has happened.

I don't know if I will be able to tell you everything, or even if it is proper to do so, but I need to share this with someone.

Your cousin Matthias came calling today. He was drunk and kept saying things about how the plantation should have been his, and that he had come to see what was going on now that Papa and Mama had ruined it. I could tell that Mama loathed him. Her mouth was pursed the whole time, and her eyes didn't blink, and even though she kept asking him to leave, he ignored her. That was bad enough but then he turned to me, and when I tried to respond to his ludicrous comments about everyone being 'insubordinate' on the plantation, he said that I was 'way too smart to catch a man'. He looked me up and down like I was his property with a detestable smirk on his face and said that I was 'real pretty, anyhow' in a way that made me shudder.

It was at that point that Mama demanded that Matthias leave. I was quite astounded because usually she doesn't express her view about anything and, as you know, lately she has spent too much time sitting on the porch and acting as if she is quite removed from our world. But today she seemed changed and told him to leave, firm and clear. It was pointless, though. He was so arrogant and acted as if she hadn't opened her mouth and marched around with a gun in his holster, taking swigs of alcohol from a canister.

As soon as he was out of earshot, Mama told me to go into town. I was a little relieved. I hated the way he kept looking at me, slurring his words, and saying I must be thinking of marrying soon, even though Mama told him I was only fifteen. But, as soon as I had saddled up my horse, setting off towards town, I thought about the papers I found in Papa's office. I thought they might at least prove to him that the plantation was left to Grandpa alone and not to his father.

I turned the horse around, heading back towards the plantation. But, Aunt, it was too late and, as soon as I rode back through the gates, I heard a terrible sound. I didn't know what it was, at first, but as I got closer, I realised that it was screams or cries, and then a loud wail, piercing and horrible, which sounded like it came from a woman. My heart was racing so much I couldn't breathe but it wasn't until I turned the corner that I saw what was going on. It turned my blood to ice, and I can barely write this without feeling nauseous and angry, all at once. Matthias was just standing there, watching James, the overseer, who had a long rope in his hand. In the middle of the yard and, strapped to a tree, was Martha.

I jumped off my horse, running as fast as I could, over towards them. I screamed at Matthias and James to stop but they just laughed in my face.

I didn't know what to do so I went over to Martha, trying to cover her with my shawl but James kept coming towards her, waving his whip, as if I wasn't there.

Tildy, Rachel and Mary were a few metres away, Tildy trembling as tears fell down her face but, every time they moved, James hit the rope on the ground in front of them.

It was then that I stood in front of James and the rope. I was sure he wouldn't hit me at least and called to Tildy to take Martha inside. Her back looked raw, and she needed to put some ointment on her wounds. 'This is my father's property,' I shouted at James, although I was shaking, but Matthias just laughed, and James didn't move one inch. I stopped them long enough, for Tildy and Rachel to rush over to try to untie the ropes but they still couldn't get past James who kept crashing down the whip, hitting their legs and feet so hard they wailed out in pain.

I didn't know what else to do but just then there was the sound of gunshot. At first, I thought it was Matthias but then I saw Mama, standing on the porch, holding a rifle. It was pointed right at Matthias and her face was set into the most frightening expression I ever saw. Aunt, Matthias just looked at her, his face scrunched up into a look of complete hatred, and then he got out his gun and walked over towards Martha. I was shaking, not sure what to do, but then Mary jumped in front of Martha, a few inches away from Matthias. I screamed at him to stop but he grabbed the rope from James. Aunt, I was sure he was going to hit her too, but Mary just stood still, her eyes ferocious balls of fire as he walked towards her.

'No, no!' I screamed at Matthias, grabbing his arm, but he threw me off.

And then there was another shot. Mama had fired the gun. The bullet must have whizzed by Matthias body, close enough that he dropped the rope on the ground. Mama didn't even blink. She just marched over to Matthias, still holding the gun. They stood across from each other for a few seconds, Mama looking at Matthias with so much contempt it made me shudder.

'Mama,' I said, scared that she would actually shoot him. 'I can prove that this is our property. All these guns will only make things worse.' But Mama didn't flicker. She just stayed, like she was frozen, as she stared at Matthias. 'The will was approved by a court,' I said. 'I saw it. Everything was left to my Grandpa . . .'

Matthias turned to me. I don't think anyone has ever looked at me like that before. Like I was absolutely nothing. 'And why would I believe a silly, spoilt fifteen-year-old girl,' he said, drawling out his voice.

'Because it's true,' I told him as firmly as I could although my face was trembling with rage. 'And because, if you don't, you'll end up going to jail. Perhaps for years.' His lip quivered. I thought he'd at least heard what I said, which gave me confidence to carry on. 'This is my parents' property, Matthias . . .and they are perceived as fine people in this community. They don't drink. They are not known as wastrels. My father is not a philanderer.' I took a chance, remembering something Mama muttered to Papa once about Matthias being a womaniser. 'It's all about perception. You know that. And there are ten witnesses here who will say you were in the wrong. Disrespecting my papa's property,' I winced, feeling my face go red. 'And his wife and daughter.'

Matthias edged towards me until he was only a metre away from me. I could sense the heat of his body, his arms stiff and his face contorted into a horrible grimace.

'You need to leave.' Mama said, still holding the gun.

'Mama,' I said. 'Put down the gun.' She didn't move at all at first, like she was frozen or trapped. 'Mama,' I said again, although my heart was pounding as she slowly lowered the

gun. Matthias forced a laugh, throwing his head back but I caught a flash of fear cross his face. 'You think you are so intelligent. So fine,' he said through gritted teeth, glaring at me and then at Mama. 'But you are nothing without this big house and those fine clothes.' He walked back to his horse. 'You remember that.'

'You go too James,' Mama said.

I thought he would be ashamed, or at least try to explain, but he just shrugged and walked to within a few inches of Mama. 'Expecting my wages,' he hissed. 'Been keeping discipline around the place for a long time – a fact your husband appreciates.'

'What do you mean?' I asked, feeling a sense of dread. 'Papa wouldn't allow that.'

But James came up so close to me that his spit landed on my cheek and said, 'You think what you want about your precious daddy, but he knows this is the only way to keep some sort of control. Turns a blind eye to what he don't see but needs to be done just the same.'

Before I went to bed, Mama put her arms around me. For a few seconds, I laid my head on her shoulder, tears falling down my face.

'You need to leave here Ruby,' Mama said.

I flinched, wondering if she knows how many times I asked you about coming to live with you. 'There is so much beauty here. But hate and fear is turning people into animals.' I nodded although I didn't know for sure if she was talking about herself or Matthias. 'And Ruby, you are not nothing. You can do something in this world. You just have to keep remembering who you are. And not give in to the expectations of those around you.'

I had been in bed for a few hours, unable to sleep with everything going around and around in my head, when the door creaked open. It was Benjamin. He came in and lay on the floor next to the bed. 'Benjamin, did you know about Papa?' I whispered. He didn't answer. But, when I woke in the morning, he was still there, lying on his side, eyes open and just staring into nothing.

Please, Iris, I don't mind what work I have to do. I just need to get out of here.

Ruby.

October 10th, 1851
Dearest Ruby,

I write this in haste after receiving your dreadful, and disturbing news. I do hope that you are alright my dear Ruby. You were brave. And you were right to use words and reason. There is so much violence. And so much hate. Sometimes I think the whole world could end up killing each other.

My cousin, Matthias, was always vile. Our father inherited the plantation from his father. Your grandfather, and Matthias's father, George, were brothers. George was given a considerable sum of money, which he promptly squandered which led to their father's decision to leave the entirety of the plantation to your grandfather.

Recognising that it did not sit well with his Christian morals, my father always intended to free the thirty-five people enslaved on his land, as soon as he felt economically able. In fact, a few seasons of poor crops left the plantation in dire financial circumstances and, although it is not an excuse for his unconscionable lack of action, he did not do as he promised. Over time, my father considered ways ideas to make the plantation more profitable, introducing different crops and selling part of the land. However, he became ill before he could complete his plan and, at the time of his death, had only freed three or four men and women. I am told that my father's last words were a wish that Theodore, your father, would do what he did not and to provide some sort of employment, if they should wish it, for all those who were freed.

In saying all this, I must take some responsibility myself. I could have done more, but, despite my good education, my father considered that, as a woman, it was not appropriate for me to run the plantation and imagined that I would marry some wealthy landowner. I did not want anything to do with it and so lost any opportunity to make any real difference by giving up my share and leaving for Boston. It seems foolish now, but, at the time, I trusted Theodore to carry out his plan, but he was a newly married, inexperienced man of twenty-six when he inherited the estate, and, to my knowledge, has not freed one person in twenty years.

I sincerely hope that you will choose to come and live here, dear Ruby, but you need to be aware that it is a modest, austere life, which Charlotte and I try to support by earning a little money from tutoring and sewing. Despite this, I would not change it. I have experienced many things and have met some quite remarkable people.

In writing this letter I realise that I have been rather remiss in sending you reading material for a while and now attach some pages from the autobiography of another great writer, Frederick Douglass, who said that 'it is easier to build strong children than to repair broken men'. He is quite an exceptional man, who was formerly enslaved himself, and I have had the pleasure of hearing him speak in his drive towards the abolition of slavery.

Keep well, Ruby.
Your affectionate aunt,
Iris

Chapter Thirty

Clover

The police officer that we spoke to about Caterina's disappearance is there in the kitchen when I come down for breakfast, smart and formal in a navy suit with dark brown hair in a ponytail.

It's been five days since Caterina appeared at the hostel, the day we got back from Winchester.

'I'm DC Winter,' the police officer reminds me.

'Have you heard anything about Caterina?' I ask.

'Not directly. But the police over in Truro are investigating a farm,' she explains. 'We received calls from a local resident who was concerned about the condition of some of the workers there.' She glances at Dad. 'Clover, did you ever see the man that Caterina was with?'

'Only at a distance. She didn't want him to see *me*.'

'Do you know where she came from? Or even why she was living in the hut?' DC Winter asks.

'She didn't say.' I shake my head slightly, feeling sick. 'I knew she was hungry. I tried to give her some food.'

'It's just a hunch, really, but we were wondering whether she escaped from the farm.'

'I know I should have asked her more. It sounds ridiculous now. But she was insistent. Every time I tried to ask her things like that she would get upset. And . . .'

'What is it?' Dad asks.

'She said that if I told anyone she might be killed – or worse.'

Dad winces.

'I know I should have told someone.'

Dad touches my shoulder, his hand remaining there. It feels nice. Not just that little bit of pressure and burst of warmth but because I feel like he's supporting me. Which makes me feel safe.

'Clover, you mustn't go anywhere near that hut,' Dad says sternly, catching up with me when I try to sneak out of the hostel later.

'I'm going for a walk,' I say. 'You can't actually expect me to concentrate on schoolwork or anything else today.' I can't stop thinking about Caterina, and every movement of the door or shrill sound of the phone makes me jump.

'Of course not,' Dad says, his face betraying his frustration, 'but I mean it, Clover. The police will look for Caterina. These people are dangerous.'

'You can't think that Caterina's dangerous. That's ridiculous.'

'Not *Caterina*, but people she might be involved with,' Dad says. 'You have to stay well away.'

'But do you think the police will actually do anything?' I ask. 'I'm not saying they won't try, but it's a needle in a haystack, isn't it?'

'Clover,' Dad says firmly. 'This isn't anyone messing around – it's *serious*.'

'OK,' I say eventually, 'I'll just go down to the town,

then.' I head towards the winding track, but I feel sick every time I think about how ill Caterina looked the last time I saw her. I'm almost at the path leading into town when I hear Dad's voice again and, when I turn around, he's a few metres behind me, his face flushed and tiny droplets of sweat on his forehead.

'I'm coming with you,' he says, lines appearing around his eyes.

'Dad,' I say, 'I'm not out on some dangerous mission – I'm going to the *library*.'

There's that sound again, that little bubble laugh.

We go to the upstairs gallery. It has floor-to-ceiling windows, and light streams through them making everything golden. 'What are you looking for?' Dad asks.

'I was going to read the last batch of letters that Grandma sent again,' I explain quietly. 'See if I can actually work out what happened.'

'Do you mind if I read them as well?' Dad asks, a little doubt in his voice.

'No, of course I don't,' I say, feeling guilty that I hadn't included him in the first place.

The creases at the edge of Dad's eyes disappear. 'Hot chocolate?' he asks.

'Yes, please.' I find a window seat and take the stack of papers out of my bag, setting them out on the table.

When Dad comes back, he gives me a little look, a frown flashing across his eyes as he sees the pile of papers, because it's *all* the letters, not just the ones I got from Grandma but the others as well, from Ruby and Mary and Iris, some of which he hasn't seen.

I can tell Dad's confused but he takes a sip of his coffee. 'I wanted to read them all again to see if I could work it all out. I thought I might have missed some clues,' I say but Dad just nods and turns the first page. We sit there for hours, reading in silence although, once or twice, I glance up from my reading and see his hands clenched so that his nails dig into his palm.

We leave the library just after five o'clock. It's still light and the sky's bright blue. 'Thank you for sharing the letters with me,' Dad says.

'I'm sorry,' I say.

'What for?'

'For trying to sneak off with them . . . I just couldn't stop thinking about Caterina and I thought you were annoyed with me.'

'About what?'

'The Caterina thing. Not telling you and everything.'

'Well, you're my daughter.'

'So?'

'So, it means that I was *worried*.' Dad smiles, but it's just a small movement of his mouth and doesn't reach his eyes. 'Walk along the beach?' he asks.

'OK,' I say, a slight breeze catching my hair. 'Who do you think R is?' I ask.

Dad shrugs. 'We only know of Ruby or Reuben. But both seem unlikely.'

'I thought maybe it was Ruby. But that doesn't make sense either – I mean, why would she tell all those things to Ruby when she was there all along?'

Dad shakes his head. 'It's all so horrific, isn't it? Although one of the worst things is the apathy.'

'What do you mean?'

'That so many people didn't *do* anything.'

'Are you talking about me with Caterina?' I ask, stopping still.

'No!' exclaims Dad. 'No, Clover.' He crouches down

on the beach, gathering up a handful of sand. Little clouds fall through his fingers. 'I'm really ashamed,' he says.

'What do you mean?'

'That I left you . . .'

I open my mouth, but nothing comes out, so we carry on walking, until we reach the cliffs, half a mile or so along the beach and turn back. 'Dad, I read your letter . . .' Something about his face as he looks at me makes me flinch. 'Dad, you left and that was it. For years.' I dare to look at him. 'I mean, whose decision was it? I never . . .'

I look away, staring towards the row of coloured beach huts because I hate looking at Dad's face and seeing that pain. But I don't finish my sentence. Something is strange about one of the beach huts. The door is slightly ajar, even though it seems too cool and early in the year. And I can see something. *Someone.*

Dad and I realise at the same time and look at each other. It's a girl.

Chapter Thirty-One

Mary

October, 1851
Dear R,

The moon looks full and ready to burst on out. I walk past the stables, just before sunset, sensing the earthy smell of heat and straw, the rustling of hay, and the low, gentle braying of horses. Abraham calmly pats one of the horses, stroking it in slow, rhythmic movements. I hear him talking to the horse as if it's a person, his gravelly voice patient and kind.

But then I see someone behind him, lurking in the shadows of the stables. 'This is Solomon,' Abraham says, as the man steps forwards and I can properly see his face. 'He's come to bring over an order from Massa McDonald's plantation.' He gives me a look, like it's important, even though his voice is light. 'He'll be staying the night. In the cabin at the end.'

After supper, we sit out on the porch. I lean into Tildy, feeling the gentle breeze swirling around my face and the music from the fiddle and tap-tapping of the drum fill my ears. And Martha's voice, moving her foot in time with the rhythm as she tells the story about Brer Rabbit and the Tar Baby, and how Brer Rabbit tricks Brer Fox with his clever words and cunning to get him thrown into the briar patch.

I know this story. I love this story. Because Brer Rabbit outsmarts Brer Fox and gets himself home.

And then I hear Abraham's voice, soft and light.

'When Israel was in Egypt's land

'Let my people go,

'Oppress'd so hard they could not stand

'Let my people go.'

I don't want to meet Martha's eyes, to acknowledge that these moments, out on the porch with Abraham's fiddle beautiful like a lark, or Tildy with her arms around me so that I lean into her just as if she were my momma and can make my heart beat with a gentle pitter-patter, will soon be over. But when I dare to look up, I see Martha, her eyes fixed and glinting, and she gives me a small nod.

Chapter Thirty-Two

Clover

I can see the girl more clearly now. The red-brown strands of her hair, and the way she's moving her head, chin up in the air as she searches around. I don't stop to think, I just run, as fast as I can, towards the hut.

'Stay back!' Dad hisses, catching up with me.

'No,' I gasp. 'It's Caterina. She trusts me.'

'You said yourself that you thought the man seemed strict. What if he's there too?'

'Dad,' I say, '*You* stay back. She'll freak if she sees you. Just let me speak to her. On my *own*.' All those times when I doubted what I should do but now I'm certain. Maybe reading about Ruby and Mary and how often when people thought about doing something but never actually did has somehow changed me.

'This is for the police,' Dad says. 'It could be dangerous.' He puts his hand on my arm, but I shake it off.

Dad tries to follow me, but he struggles to move quickly on the soft sand, and I reach the door before he can catch up. I motion to him to stay back. To my surprise, he stops.

The lock has been forced so the door doesn't close properly but I still knock. 'Caterina,' I call gently. She doesn't answer but I stay still. I can't hear anything, but I know she's in there.

'Caterina,' I say again, pushing gently on the door. It doesn't open. Caterina must have blocked it with something. 'It's me.' There's a small movement inside, a creak in the floor. 'I need to speak to you,' I say again. 'Caterina, it's OK. Really. *Please* open the door . . .'

I wait, listening for any noise, but all I hear is the rhythmic sound of waves, until there's some whispering, two voices – one low and slightly gruff – and then the door creaks open. It's just a few centimetres but it's enough to see a wisp of hair falling over wide green eyes.

'Caterina!' I gasp. I glance over at Dad but he's still some distance away, moving anxiously from foot to foot. I push on the door until it's wide enough that I can see Caterina properly. She's standing completely still, matted hair hanging limp to her shoulders, her face paler and thinner than I remembered. She reminds me of the crumpled ragdoll Mum made me when I was four.

'We were really worried about you'.

'Who was? Who is "we"?' Caterina asks, her terrified eyes darting around her.

'Me and, well, my dad,' I say, biting my lip as I realise my mistake.

'No!' Caterina exclaims, trying to push the door closed. 'You *promised*.'

I force my foot in the door and, when I see Dad move towards us, I hold up my hand to tell him to stop. 'Caterina,' I plead, 'It's alright. He promised he won't come any closer.'

'Why did you tell him?'

'I didn't. I mean, after you came to the hostel people asked questions. And then you disappeared,' I explain. 'Why did you leave the hut so suddenly?'

Caterina stares at me almost blankly. 'We thought we'd been found,' she says.

'Come with me. You're not well.' I hold out my hand, but she just stays still, shivering and her eyes enormous on her small face, until eventually she takes my hand.

I try to tug her a little, but her feet stay fixed to the ground. 'You don't understand,' she says, but she starts to cough, her shoulders trembling and eyes watering as if she's choking.

'Look,' I say, more loudly this time because that sound in her chest is scary. 'My dad won't come over unless you say it's OK, but he's a really good person . . . He'll help you.' I suddenly realise that it's true. 'You don't have to be scared . . .And if you don't want him to get involved. That's fine. I will help you. Whatever it is . . .but you need to leave here. And now.' My voice seems loud, now, but I don't want to leave this time. I don't want to just act as if everything is going to be fine. I need to do something, whatever it takes. 'Come on,' I say as definitely as I can.

'But you don't understand,' Caterina says quietly. She lets go of my hand, opening the door wider until I can see the small space, the few blankets lying on the floor and a camping kettle on a shelf.

And in the corner is the man. Not strong and scary but all bones and grey. He has a deep scar on the left side of his face and his hands are quivering.

Caterina takes his arm. 'This is my uncle,' she says. She glances at him, as if she's asking him a question. 'And it's him that's scared. Not me.'

I stand still, waiting while Caterina talks to her uncle

in a language I don't understand until she holds his sleeve, steering him towards the door. He's so weak that he doesn't resist. I give him a little smile, but his eyes are blank and empty. I don't say anything else. I just gently take his left arm and try to help him out of the door.

Dad brings over steaming cups of sugary tea and sandwiches made with thick hunks of granary bread. Caterina and her uncle sit still in the deep armchairs of the hostel lounge. Her uncle's eyes dart around every few seconds but he seems too weak to move.

DC Winter arrives half an hour later, together with another police officer – a young, energetic man whose eyes flicker from Caterina to her uncle and to us, like he's confused.

'We need to take Anton and Caterina to a doctor,' DC Winter says, glancing over at Caterina's uncle, whose face seems fixed to the floor.

'Can't they stay here?' I ask.

'No, Clover,' she replies gently, 'Caterina and Anton need medical attention. They need clothes and food. And they need to feel – and to *be* – safe.'

I try to smile at Caterina, but her face looks blank and empty. I thought everything would be fine once she was off the heath. Somewhere warm with food and medicines. But she just looks sad. And alone.

'OK?' DC Winter asks, until Caterina nods, a tiny movement.

'Wait a minute,' I say, darting upstairs to my room, three steps at a time. I search the shelves for a book and dig out some coloured pencils and paper from the drawer before dashing back downstairs. 'So that you'll have something to do,' I say, handing the things over to Caterina.

'Thank you,' she says, a brief look of surprise in her eyes, so that they almost twinkle.

It feels strange once they've gone. DC Winter phones an hour later. She says they're both undernourished, and that Caterina has a bad chest infection, but she'd been given antibiotics and a safe place to stay and will be fine.

Ms Delauney, Dad and I play cards for hours, until, too exhausted to carry on, we eventually trudge up to bed. When I go upstairs, I see a parcel. It's the second batch of papers that Grandma promised, wrapped in brown paper and leaning against my door.

I peel back some of the outer layer of paper. 'What is it?' Dad asks.

'It's more letters from Mary,' I say, my heart giving a little lift.

Dad hovers outside the door while I brush my teeth.

'Strange day,' Dad says, when I come out. 'A *difficult* day . . .'

'Yep,' I say.

'But I'm really proud of you, Clover.'

He has a layer of tears over his eyes. 'But it was my fault in the first place,' I say, 'I knew that she was on the heath and cold and hungry . . . so I had to find a way to help her.'

Dad wraps his arms around me, and I can smell a faint mixture of sweat and laundry powder. 'I get it,' he says simply.

I open the door to my room. I don't know if I want to talk about it anymore. I feel exhausted and upset. And happy we have found Caterina and her uncle, all at the same time.

'I think I need to go to bed,' I say.

'OK,' Dad says. 'Clover are you OK?' he asks.

'Yes,' I say starting to close the door but Dad's still looking at me. 'You know, I thought that everything had ended with Mum dying,' I say, feeling a little croak in my throat. 'I couldn't imagine what any future would look like . . .but this evening, even though it was really sad seeing Caterina and her uncle so ill, I looked around and saw you and Ms Delauney and Caterina and realised how much more I have in my life too.' I swallow. 'I still wish Mum was here . . .but for the first time, I started thinking about the future.'

'And is there anything good in there?' Dad asks, quickly hugging me.

'Yep,' I say, listening to the rhythm of his heart as I try not to cry.

Chapter Thirty-Three

Mary

October, 1851
Dear R,

I'm wearing two layers of clothes as I lie wedged between Martha and Rachel, listening to the owl somewhere out flying free in the air and the gentle rattle of the windows. I'm certain I won't sleep, but some time in the night, the branches on the roof turn into what sounds like a gentle tapping rhythm and I drift off, slipping into a world of faces and voices.

I wake up to Martha prodding my shoulder with her long fingers. 'Mary. We have to go!'

My heart is pounding but I crawl out from under the blanket, my legs numb as I stand up. I cling to Martha's hand as she slowly creaks open the door and then starts running, in little light springs, to the fence.

'Who shall I look for?' I ask between breaths.

'Solomon, of course,' she says, hugging me quickly. 'Now you make sure you do what we all dream of doing.' She squeezes my hand so tight it hurts. 'Be safe.'

'Martha,' I say, my voice cracking at the edges, 'tell Tildy I won't forget her.'

'She knows what she mean to people,' Martha says quietly before zigzagging back.

For a few seconds my heart beats faster, as I wait in the shadows of the tree. Every sound is like a footstep, the owls hooting like a scream, distant crickets chirping rhythmically in the grass, with small insects biting and crawling over my feet. Just when my heart feels like it might burst, I hear a rustling sound.

'This way,' a voice rasps out, as a face emerges into the light of the moon. *I recognise him from earlier. Solomon, eyes wide and round and a jagged scar line on the side of his face which curves from his left ear towards his lip.*

'Keep quiet and just follow me,' Solomon whispers. *We scuttle low and quiet through the woods, every crunch under our feet making my heart stop.* *'You hear anything, jump down there,'* he says, pointing to the line of ditches bordering the fields.

I know this route. It's the way towards town. I'd somehow imagined that we would be going someplace else, heading to the safety of woods, perhaps, but here I feel like a hare running scared in the fields. And it feels too obvious. And too easy to be caught which makes me think of Ned and Rachel and the horrible tales of people hanging, cords tight round their necks.

'Stay here,' Solomon whispers sharply, waving his arms at me to keep down. *I look around because we are still out in the open field, but when I look east, I see the church. I crouch low in a ditch, curling myself tight into a ball as I hold my breath, partly in terror, but also from the stench of something dead – a bird or animal, rotting in the ditch – which still lingers in the air, circling around my nostrils and pricking my eyes.*

Solomon creeps up the church steps. For a few seconds, it's as if he's on a stage and I worry that the whole town will see him, but then a door opens a fraction. Solomon darts back over to me. He grabs my sleeve, holding his finger to his lips, and gently tugs me to my feet. I mimic his movements, my heart racing as I scurry up the stairs of the church. I have a horrible feeling deep in my stomach that we have been set up somehow and, for a few seconds, I wish more than anything in the world that I was back lying in the cabin between Martha and Rachel, but then the heavy church door creaks open and Solomon pushes me inside.

'Good luck,' he whispers urgently.

A dim, flickering candle lights my way, making shadows dance on the walls. I can't see the face of the man I follow, and I stay a few steps behind him, trying to keep my feet light, as I glide across the cold floor. The man hands me a candle, pulling back a table. There's a door, hidden in the ground and, when I look down, I see what looks like a gaping hole below me. I shudder, thinking that nothing on earth could make me go down into that space, which would be like being buried alive or dropped into a dungeon or coffin, but someone reaches up their arms and carries me gently down, like a feather floating on the air, before the trapdoor closes above me.

I can't breathe. Between the darkness and a stark stench of excrement, I pant between little breaths, trying to take in enough air, but my throat feels dry. 'It's just for tonight,' someone whispers beside me. 'There are slats in the ceiling; don't worry. Calm down and you'll be able to breathe . . .' At least the voice is kind.

I look up above me, making out the tiny lines of crosses, tiny slivers of light and air in the floor of the church, so I stay still, trying to breathe, gentle and slow. Gradually my eyes start to make out a shadow, then a shape, slowly forming – a man of about sixty with weathered skin.

'I was at Massa Bolt's,' he explains and then he adds in a low voice, 'I remember you.'

In the small glow, I can just make out his wiry, greying hair and creases that slowly travel around his face as he speaks, like the patterns on the ground created by the movement of the clouds or the shadow of a tree shaking gently in the breeze.

Toby. 'You played the spoons,' I murmur.

He laughs. 'I certainly did. Tapping out the rhythm to the songs played on that old fiddle.' But then he pauses. 'Mary.' His voice rasps out the words. 'I wasn't around at the Bolt place so much with all the coming and going to Massa Worthington's property, but I remember your momma real well,' he says. 'She spoke like it was poetry or song all the time.'

The tears begin to prick my eyes, so I clench my fist because, if I start crying, I might never stop.

'I know where your brother Reuben went,' he says. 'Hannah looked after your brother real good after you left. I was loaned out to Massa Worthington over in Wessex County again as he needed extra help with his animals. But Massa run into hard times. Drinking and gambling money away all the time. Couldn't keep the plantation going.'

I feel sick. I should have told Ruby or Benjamin about Reuben sooner. I hold my breath, counting until he reaches the part that I need to hear. 'Massa Bolt clung on to all his best cotton pickers but sold the rest. Quick as he can sold off Reuben and all those young'uns. Hannah screamed so hard when they took Reuben away I thought her heart would properly break. She loved that boy.'

'Where's Reuben now?' I whisper, remembering how he gripped my fingers so tight that sometimes his little soft nails would leave a horseshoe shape in the palms of my hands.

'Taken off to Kentucky, they say. Big old plantation.'

I look at Toby, my eyes finally able to see the angle of his chin, and the whites of his eyes. He licks his lips, which are cracked and dry from dust and sun.

'Toby,' I ask, 'do you know where he is? Exactly, I mean.'

'Folks say he ain't far from the Ohio River. Folks say the plantation so close you can just walk on over the river. Wade in and cross without people noticing.'

'Is that true?' I ask, suddenly suspicious.

'I believe that people escape from there.'

'How long you been down here then?' I ask.

'Two days . . . Becoming easy to run away. Massa Bolt clean out of money. He let some of the overseers go but still drinking all the time. Rumour is he won't have enough money to pay them paddyrolls to chase after us, although mean enough to make damned sure that he tries, but even an old man like me manage to escape . . . Anyhow, Mary, before you sleep – and you better go right on down and do that or you won't be able to walk tomorrow – I'll tell you the practical things. As you can probably tell from that terrible odour, the toilet is over in that far corner in that bucket. I can't see nothing in this light and my hearing ain't so good neither, so don't you feel embarrassed.'

I won't need it. My mouth is dry as I haven't drunk or eaten anything for hours, too scared that Solomon would arrive when I had rushed off to the outhouse or that I would slow us down.

He wets his fingers and snaps out the candle, a little whirl of smoke floating in the air before the darkness returns. 'You better get some sleep . . . That knock come in the morning you have to be gone quick as anything.'

Chapter Thirty-Four

Mary

October, 1851
Dear R,

I don't know how long I sleep before I hear a rapping sound. I scramble to my feet just as the trapdoor in the ceiling opens.

A woman pulls me gently up steps I didn't see the night before, handing me a tin cup full of cold milk, which I drink immediately, and a chunk of bread I put in my pocket. 'You need to go now,' Toby whispers frantically.

'You're not coming?' I ask, confused.

'I'm on the next train, Mary,' he says with a small laugh. 'I wasn't expected. Jumped off a cart when Massa too drunk to notice and went to the nearest safehouse I knew about.' He laughs a low laugh. 'Don't you waste a single breath feeling sorry for me, Miss Mary. This still a whole lot better than lifting a finger for that devil-man, Bolt.'

The woman tugs at my sleeve. 'Come on!' she hisses. I glance back at Toby and then follow her outside, trying to mirror her movements as she stops and starts through the dry grass, looking around her every few metres, before we risk another burst. I crouch down low, keeping as still as I can, listening for sounds but there's just the rustling of birds and small animals. After a minute or so, I feel a gentle pull on my sleeve and I have to run, my feet light, towards the group of trees twenty metres in the distance.

When we reach them, I look at the woman properly. She's tall and strong. 'I'm Ruth,' she says. 'Don't stop now,' she whispers urgently, 'just follow me. We need to get to the next place . . . We got an hour until it's fully light and it's five miles away, so we need to hurry.'

We walk quickly, further and further through the trees, tripping over roots until, after a few hours when the sun is getting higher and brighter in the sky, we reach a shack deep, deep in the woods. It's mouldy and damp and I can hear the scratching of insects and mice. 'You'll need to stay here until nightfall and then walk twenty miles towards Savannah.'

'I thought we might be going towards the Ohio River,' I say.

'You any idea how many miles that is from here?! Your best chance is a boat from Savannah, going along the coast to Boston. There are a few people willing to turn a blind eye to stowaways.'

'Why would they do that?'

She looks at me for a few seconds before she gives a little nod of her head. 'Not all white folks bad. Up north, you gonna be fine,' she says, although her mouth slightly twists. 'Not saying that everyone going to treat you like their brother or sister, but a few good people still.'

My eyes widen. 'Ruth, aren't you scared that you won't get back home? That you'll be caught?'

'I've been lucky. I can read and write, get some work and a little respect . . . But I got to the point where I just couldn't live like that. It would mean ignoring everything

happening down here. So, every so often I come back, try to help some of my brothers and sisters, let them know how it feels to cross into a place where you get to be treated almost human.'

She strides to the middle of the room, scraping around on the floor amidst the leaves and mud until she prises open a door. It's a hole, four feet deep and four feet long.

'When you hear a noise, anything you don't know what – animal, bird, person – you go down there and be silent.'

I look at the space. Just to fit into it I'd have to pull my legs in tight and then stay still, waiting for what might be hours until whoever it is eventually leaves. I shudder.

'Next person coming will knock on the door like this.' Ruth taps out a rhythm.

I nod. 'Where are you going?' I whisper, terrified to be left alone again.

'Back to get Toby . . . He couldn't come this way. Too difficult for him to travel that far.' She frowns. 'He needs to go through the safehouses on the railroad . . . as long as they're actually safe.'

'You'll be able to tell from the symbols on the quilts?'

'That, and songs like special codes,' she says. 'Most white folks think we all stupid, but don't know that most have been fooling them for years with their stories.'

I think about Brer Rabbit and Brer Fox, how Momma and Pete and Abraham would laugh fit to burst at some of the tricks that Brer Rabbit used – how he fooled Brer Fox into letting him humiliate him by riding him like a horse through town, and Pete would exclaim, slapping his thigh hard, 'Imagine if that really was Massa Bolt. That would be the absolute best sight in the whole world!'

But then I remember how all the white folks sat at the front of the church as if God would think they were more special, even though they could be really mean.

'Doesn't the reverend know that people are staying in the church? Doesn't he hear people downstairs?'

She looks at me. 'Course he knows. Who do you think gave you the bread and milk?'

It's night-time again before I hear the distinct sound of footsteps. Every little creak of the tree branches crashing about on the wooden shack roof made me jump all day, but this time there's a slow cracking over dry twigs, until the sounds stop at the door. I know I should go into the hole, but I just can't, so I crouch down in the corner behind a wooden table instead, my heart pounding. I wait for a few minutes, wishing I'd climbed into that space, even if it would feel like being buried alive, because anything would be better than waiting for those heavy steps to reach the door.

Eventually the footsteps stop, so the person must be there, just standing still and staring at the front of the door. My heart is racing so much I think I might be sick, or pass out, but the silence seeps into seconds, only broken by an owl hooting high in the trees outside.

I curl up as small as I can, still and quiet, until finally I hear it. Knock. Knock, rap, rap. It's the rhythm Ruth showed me.

The door opens. 'You here?' a voice whispers. 'You here?'

For a few seconds I stay still, my hands sweaty and my heart throbbing.

'Mary.'

I crawl out of my little space.

I try to clear my dry throat and eventually whisper, 'I'm here.'

It's a man of about thirty. His mouth moves into a smile that gets wider and wider.

'I'm Samson,' he says. 'We have to go.' But then he looks at me and my terrified face and grabs my hand, giving it a little shake. 'You're alright now, Miss Mary . . .'

Chapter Thirty-Five

Ruby

October 25th, 1851
Dear Aunt Iris,

Mary has gone. Ever since that dreadful day she saw Reuben, I couldn't shake the feeling that she might try to escape.

Martha, who speaks to me a little now, says I'm wrong. She says that Mary's desire to be free was always there and that everyone would escape if they could.

Mary left two nights ago without a word or a goodbye. We found out in the morning when she did not appear in the kitchen. Tildy just stood there silent as I asked question after question, although I thought I caught a small smile alongside the shining of her tears.

When he found out, Benjamin looked right at Papa, his eyes burning and said, 'I'm glad,' but he slept in my room that night. I heard him sneak in and lay a mat on the floor under the window.

I hope Mary followed the north star that she talked about and somehow reached the place her momma always dreamed about her going. I hope she finds her brother and can tell him her stories, chin up and eyes shining. But, Aunt Iris, I cannot tell you how lonely it feels sitting in the room with no friends or dreams, except those within the pages of an atlas.

Your loving niece,
Ruby

Chapter Thirty-Six

Mary

October, 1851
Dear R,

We trudge along for at least six hours, until we eventually stop to rest, leaning against the rough bark of a tree. The branches are twisted and bent, and they're crawling with ants, which run onto my shoulders and up my arms. 'You think anyone knows about my escape?' *I ask Samson, as we sip a little water.*

'I reckon so, but I've been told that Mr Finch unlikely to send any paddyrolls out for a while.' *My stomach is empty and keeps gurgling.* 'Eat slow,' *Samson says, handing me a fist-sized chunk of dry bread.* 'Anyway, Mary, if we have any chance at all of getting that boat we need to walk fast while it's dark.'

My feet are scratched to ribbons already, scraped by every movement from the dry branches. 'Are you leaving me there?' *I ask.* 'At the boat?'

'No, I'm going with you,' *he says.* 'This time I'm going back to my family. My girl is near two and I want to be there when she's proper talking. Already walking,' *he says with a hint of pride.*

'But my brother Reuben is on a plantation in Kentucky,'

I say. 'I was thinking about maybe going along one of those railroad routes. He's near the Ohio River. They say it's easy enough to get him across.'

'You gone mad! Can't go so many miles on foot, dodging and ducking around for weeks on end. Even if you make it that far, and I think you won't, you gotta somehow contact your brother.' He gives me a little look of sympathy, 'How old is he?'

'Eight,' I say.

'You're no use to anyone if you don't get to the North. Can't do nothing here . . .' But his voice is softer when he says, 'There are important people in New York and Boston and Philadelphia. People who don't believe that this terrible thing people been doing for hundreds of years like God is on their side is right.' He taps my arm. 'You gotta take this freedom. Use your head and voice and do what's best for you, and your brother. You gotta look forwards, Mary.'

We walk for two more hours. I struggle to hold back the tears even though I try not to think about Reuben too much. Or Tildy or Martha or Ruby, focusing instead on the sounds of the birds, and their song. I know it's near morning. The light will come up soon and then we'll be obvious, all lit up in the pink and yellow light of dawn. But a few miles before we get to the boat, my foot snags on something on the ground. I try to catch my step, but end up falling and, when I open my eyes, I'm lying flat on the earth, prickly twigs sticking into the middle of my back. Samson is waving his hand in front of my face in rapid movements, trying to fan me. 'You alright there?' he says, creases criss-crossing his brow.

I nod, touching my head and face. My left cheek has rough lines etched across it, and my head has a bump.

'Took a tumble on that root over there and fell headlong into the tree. Bumped your head quite bad, I think. You've been

out for a while.' He holds my head gently in his palm, giving me sips of water, but my head is still spinning, and little dots jump up in front of my eyes. 'The boat,' I say, remembering suddenly.

'We'll just get there when we can,' he says. 'Can you try to stand up? Not long until dawn and it's a good two miles further to the docks.'

I try to stand but everything swirls around me and my legs feel so heavy that it's like walking through a swamp every time I try to take a step forward. 'Take it slow,' Samson says, giving me another sip of water but my head is crashing, and I see the lines over his forehead like ripples of water. 'Alright, Mary,' he says, 'we need a different plan. Too late to go to the docks now anyhow, I reckon. By the time we get there it will be buzzing and, even though I have papers, I don't much want to come across a patteroller.'

'What we gonna do then?'

He pauses. 'Think the minister of the Savannah African Church will help us out,' he says.

We take small steps, me leaning on Samson's arm. My head is still a blur, but the light is creeping down through the leaves up above us. After the shelter of the trees, I give a little shudder at what's ahead. It feels so exposed.

'Keep your head,' Samson mutters, and leads me into the open ground.

Chapter Thirty-Seven

Mary

October, 1851
Dear R,

Samson comes back to the Savannah African Church early the next evening. My head is still throbbing, and the hours have passed in a strange whirl. The minister's wife, Sarah, comes in twice, bringing a drink and a piece of cornbread and sweet-smelling burdock tea for the bump on my head.

'How are you free?' I ask her.

'I was born on a plantation near here, but my Momma was a wonderful cook. People far and wide heard about her cooking and she was paid to make meals for grand dinners in all these different houses. After ten years of saving every last nickel, she managed to earn enough money to buy herself and her three children free.' She sighs. 'Don't think you'll be getting the boat from Savannah any time soon,' she says. 'Crawling with the meanest patterollers I ever saw. Checking the boats too because of the big escape from a plantation thirty mile away two week back. Soon as they look at you, they'll have you beaten and strung up so tight you can't breathe.'

'What shall we do then?' Samson asks.

'Only one thing you can really do,' she says.

'What's that?' Samson asks.

'You better get to Charleston.'

'Can you walk?' Samson asks me, frowning.

'I reckon so,' I say, struggling to my feet although my legs tremble just as soon as I put one foot in front of the other.

'You might have to,' he says. 'We gotta try to get near ten miles before morning.'

We walk along back roads, Samson's eyes darting around. Every sound makes me shiver although usually it is nothing, but sometimes Samson stops still, his eyes wide as he waves his hand in frantic motions to tell me to jump into a ditch.

My head is crowded full of Reuben and Tildy, Martha and Ruby. And I can't shift an image of Benjamin, which bothers me even more, and the clear steady way that his eyes always focused on me, not blinking or glancing away.

It's easier when we are back in the trees, although we must tread lightly, trying not to crunch on the twigs and loose branches scattered on the ground. Every few hours we stop, sitting on tree trunks, to sip water and take a few mouthfuls of cornbread. 'What kinda life do you think your daughter will have in New York?' I ask. 'Do you think she'll learn to read and go to school?'

'Hope so,' he says. 'Don't want her having my life, scraping around and always having to accept second place.'

'Even in the North?'

'Yep, even in the North . . .' Samson looks at me. 'Still much better, though. And anyway, you'll be free.'

The sun is rising when we reach the outskirts of a town. There are a few houses, spaced out, with small grass verges at the front of a veranda. It's quiet except for the soft scurry of animals the sounds of birds high in the tall trees that line the road.

'This the house,' Samson says, his head jerking in little movements as he looks around. 'Stay back, though.' He darts over, knocking at the door so lightly it could be the sound of a bird scuttling in the earth.

A quilt is hanging at the window, and I think back to those lessons with Martha, scratching images into the dusty dirt by the old oak. I recognise the shapes that look like a window, surrounded by rectangles, or planks of wood, almost like a log cabin. A safehouse.

Samson beckons me over and I run as low and light as I can across the road. A woman of about thirty shows us to a pantry. She has golden hair tied back into a bun and looks at me curiously as she brings us a blanket each and some milk and pieces of chicken and bread. 'It's not much,' she mutters, 'but I hope it helps a bit with the hunger.'

'Thank you,' I say, unable to hold back a little gasp at the smell of warm food.

'You need to stay until tomorrow night and then head to the next place. Use the outhouse in the yard now and then be absolutely silent. You understand?'

I nod, a little scared of the fierceness of her eyes – the colour of fresh green leaves before they have settled into that deep, moist colour. But then she looks at me kindly. 'What's your name?'

'Mary.'

'And how old are you?'

'Near sixteen,' I say.

'Haven't you got a mama?' she asks.

'Yes,' I say, 'and a brother, Reuben, who is eight, but my momma was taken away by speculators three years ago.'

And then I see a mass of material, in gentle folds in the

corner, billowing like shallow waves. One of the designs leaps out at me, a combination of triangles I don't recognise, turning like a wheel, or the wisps of a dandelion whirling around.

'What's that pattern?' I ask quietly.

'Flying geese,' she says. 'It means to go north. They're birds . . .'

'Oh yes,' I say, suddenly seeing the movement and the shapes of the wings. Something makes me think of a day in late summer when the sun was hot and constant and Momma told me stories in her treacle-smooth voice, under a sycamore maple tree as the seeds spiral down.

'I thought it was a sycamore,' I say. 'My momma used to tell me stories in its shade.'

She shakes her head, her eyes suddenly ferocious. 'This can't last. This terrible thing can't last.' And then she almost glides through the door and closes it softly behind her.

We leave the next day, walking for hours until my legs and arms are aching so much, I think they'll drop off. I don't speak as we follow the line of the ditch, only stopping for a few seconds, twice to rest and have a few sips of water. In the darkness, the wind rustles loud in the trees and I breathe more softly when the sun starts to rise. Samson studies the sky, but the clouds cover the sun. 'Don't usually walk without something to guide us,' he says.

'Moss grows on the north side,' I say, remembering something Tildy told me, missing her so much that tears dart into my eyes, until I think about the stifling sensation of the heat of the kitchen and the cramped, horrible cabin. And Martha's back with its spider's web of lines and scars.

'It's a good thing you got brains sharp as knives,' Samson says, which makes me think of Martha again.

We walk for six or seven more miles, until my feet are

rubbing, and the soles of my shoes are so worn down that I feel every stone under my feet, until Samson jerks to a stop, his eyes so wide I gasp.

I listen and hear it too, in the distance. 'Dogs,' I mouth to him, my heart racing. He gestures to me to hide behind the tree but, as I press myself against the nearest one a few metres from the path, I hear another noise. Horses' hooves.

'The river,' Samson whispers. 'The dogs won't be able to get any scent.'

My heart is pounding as we run, bent low towards the water, trying to slip into the river without making a sound.

'Keep moving as fast as you can,' he whispers, panic in his eyes as a dog barks, so close now that I have to crouch real low in the water. Something slithers past my leg, but I wade as quickly as I can until the dogs are too near to risk moving any further.

We stay close to the bank, listening in silence to what sounds like three or four voices. Samson raises his finger to his lips, but the dogs are sniffing around fifty or so metres away, their barking becoming more and more frenzied. Samson gestures to me to sink lower and lower until, just when I can see a horse coming round the corner, I take a deep breath and put my head full under the water.

I hold my breath as long as I can until I need to come up for air. I lift my head just a fraction above the surface. The dogs are gone at least. But, when I look around, I can't see Samson.

I start to wade, slowly and as noiselessly as I can for a few steps. It looks safe, but that makes me nervous too and my body is trembling now as I listen for any small sound.

I start to move into the shallower part of the water but, when I am near the edge, something stops me.

A sharp, loud sound, so close it makes me jump.

It's the sound of metal clinking.

I sink back down into the water, my eyes darting around. There's something moving. I watch, hoping it's an animal, but then I hear a rustling of trees, and someone comes out into the light. It's a man – a thick belt around his waist, and a gun in his hand.

A patteroller.

One of the dogs is sniffing around him but he hasn't seen me, so I edge backwards – slowly, slowly – trying to sink back down into the water, wishing I'd stayed there in the first place and hadn't been so impatient. My heart is pounding so hard I think he'll hear it or sense my breathing. His dog is frantic, barking and pulling at him, but he ignores it and, when the dog doesn't stop, he kicks it hard with his boot so that it leaps back, whimpering.

I don't know what to do. I have no idea where Samson is. But as I stay, frozen, I think about Samson and Ruth and Solomon. All those risks they took. All that way we've walked. I can't let it be for nothing.

I take as big a breath as I can, going back under the water and then I wait. When my lungs feel like they might burst, I come up again.

The man is gone, so I wade along the river, staying within a few inches of the bank. 'Samson,' I whisper, feeling sicker and sicker and wanting to open my voice and yell. But I can't.

The dogs must still be nearby and every sound of a bird in the leaves sounds like footsteps. But then I see a movement, eyes bright and staring, under the roots of a tree on the edge of the bank, using it as a shelter. Samson. Smiling.

We stay at the Quaker House for three days. Elizabeth and Michael Herbert are kind. They give me slate and pencils, picture books and a needle and thread to embroider so that

I have something to do. I still spend hours going to my story inside, though, trying to invent a world with trees covered in pink magnolias where Reuben can explore and look for bugs and butterflies all day.

Walking seems easier when we move on. Maybe I've got used to it. We sleep in the woods, hidden between branches, although every sound of a bird moving or small mammals running around makes my heart stop.

'Mary, now you need to listen good, now,' Samson says, suddenly grasping my arm. 'We're going to be into Charleston soon. Always people around the docks early morning, unloading, loading. You just gotta walk tall if you see anyone, look confident and smile a little. You my sister. We just free people from the North. Doing a little business and then returning home to our families. I got papers – we just gotta hope they don't ask for yours.'

We pass warehouses in dull red and grey brick until we reach the dock. My heart is beating so fast I think it might explode. Samson glances around, stopping by a pile of crates, wooden with bold black writing on the side of each one, stacked four high, gesturing to me to move behind the crates, so that we are hidden from the people on the dock.

'Now, Mary, we not gonna do any running. If we're seen, we gotta pretend that we have every right to go on that boat. That we are legitimate.' He looks at me, his forehead creasing into a horizontal line which, for a moment, looks like a scar. 'Now, not saying that I want the world to see us exactly, just if they do, you not look like you scared scurrying around or anything. So, once the men with those papers over there go inside, we'll walk towards the boat – see, it's just on the other side of that one. Anyone see us dodging around and they'll know for sure we're not to be there.'

It's at least ten long minutes before the tall man with a

black beard becomes agitated, throwing his arms around as he argues with the man in the office. Samson watches for thirty or so seconds more and then he nods his head, moving low and quick until we reach a second set of crates. And suddenly, right in front of us, is the boat.

'Now we need to get on this boat without anyone noticing us,' Samson says firmly.

I wait, completely still, until I see Samson move and then I pace forward, behind Samson whose feet are nimble and light despite his strong frame. My heart is pounding so much I think it must be making a noise. Until we have to stop and wait again. I watch Samson, with his finger to his lips, until he darts to the boat, jumping over the side and falling with a soft thud. I follow, managing to hook my foot over the side. We creep around to a set of stairs, going two storeys down to a small doorway. When Samson has managed to prise open the door to half an arm's length, he tilts his head to me to go inside. 'Hide in the corner, under that blanket. Make sure you get a little air,' Samson whispers, 'but you hear anything at all, stay still.'

There's a rustle, rats or mice running around, and a heavy odour of rotting flesh – a dead animal, maybe, or damp. I pick my way through boxes to the corner, seeing the dusty blanket, its smell reaching my nose. I don't know whether I can keep my stomach from churning, but I curl myself into a ball, crawling under the small, broken table, and laying the blanket over the top. I wonder if there's ever been air in this place, and my arms and hands are shaking now – with fear or sickness, I don't know. I take a few breaths, until my chest slows down, focusing instead on the smell of my hands, of grass and leaves.

And then I think of Ruth, strong and confident. And free. And of Momma, her words suddenly loud in my ears, so that it makes my heart and head and fingers tingle a little.

Because, even flying above those fields, in my imagination, I know that all those places from the sky look beautiful and serene, even though, really, they are flooded red with blood.

The tears start to fall, slowly. I don't even try to stop them. I just try to shut out the noises as it gets lighter and busier outside. The laughter of a woman, the boom of a man talking about politics, a child crying and then running, small footsteps on the wood. Men and women and children in fine clothes with lace and parasols. And somewhere, within that whirl of words and sounds and the uneven rhythm of my breath, I fall asleep.

Chapter Thirty-Eight

Clover

May

'Are we all ready?' DC Winter asks. We're in a room at the police station. It's plain and windowless.

Caterina glances over at me nervously. I don't really like the room either. It smells musty and is airless, but I see Caterina chewing her lip and her hands opening and closing under the desk, so I try to catch her eye to smile at her.

'We have Marion Watson, social worker, here, and Clover and Isaac James who are here at Caterina's request,' DC Winter says into the recording machine.

'I'm ready,' Caterina whispers.

'Sorry?' DC Winter asks. 'Can you repeat that for the tape?'

Caterina coughs a little. 'I'm ready,' she says again, this time more loudly.

'Why don't you start from when you first came to live with your uncle?' DC Winter suggests softly.

Caterina's hands are on the table. She doesn't speak,

staring down at her fingers.

'Caterina?' DC Winter says. 'I know this is hard . . .'

'Sorry,' she says, again with a little dry cough. But then she fixes her wide green eyes on a point a few metres ahead of her and, slowly, begins to speak.

'I didn't go to school that much. It was three miles away, which I had to walk, and most of the teachers didn't seem to care. Except one female teacher who smiled a lot and told me I was a bright girl. My uncle wanted me to go to school. He would shake his head when he came back from work and I had been at home all day, helping my aunt cook or sitting on the swing, staring up at the sky. But, in the winter, the walk was terrible. Sometimes it was icy cold. I mean, *absolutely freezing*, not like here. You had to wear three pairs of socks and a scarf up around your mouth and, even then, you'd still feel like the wind would bite off your fingers and toes.' She pauses, and I grip her hand until she gives a little smile. 'But my uncle lost his job and then there were all these arguments. My aunt left – she went back to stay with her family in the city.' She glances around. 'I suppose my uncle must have just felt a bit desperate – it sounds stupid now, but I think he just really hoped it was true.'

'Thought what was true, Caterina? What was the arrangement? As far as you were aware?' DC Winter asks.

'They said they would get us good life. I would help out around the house, do some cleaning in return for language lessons.'

'And your uncle believed them?'

'I suppose he *wanted* to believe it,' she says. 'You see, there was no work where we were. My aunt was barely scraping a living even in the city. Everything was about learning English, trying to get to, well . . . somewhere else.

America or Britain, maybe.' She looks down towards her hands, now in her lap. Tears prickle at her eyes, but she wipes them roughly away. 'Anyway, I *did* learn English . . . but it was just from them having the television on all day or barking orders at me in English. They'd lived here for ten years, and it was the only language we both understood.'

'Do you know who made the arrangement with your uncle?'

'He said that it was the man named Kristof. He was the really mean one.'

'In what sense?'

'He *looked* mean. He snarled when he looked at you and his eyes seemed dead.' She hesitates. 'I think Kristof knew the people in the house I was sent to really well . . .' Her eyes flicker around, almost panicked. She reminds me of a young animal. 'My uncle won't get into any trouble, will he?'

'No,' DC Winter reassures her.

'It wasn't so bad. They didn't beat me or anything . . .' But then she stops, and I see her hands trembling, a tremor that travels through her arms to her shoulders until she starts to cry, tears falling down her face in small streams.

I move my chair closer, so I can put my arms around her.

'Do you want to have a break?' DC Winter asks, handing Caterina a glass of water and a stack of tissues, but she shakes her head vigorously, pulling away from me although her hand is still clinging on to mine.

'I just want to finish . . . and then maybe forget it all,' she says in English, 'if I *can* . . .'

'Of course,' DC Winter says.

'They locked me in a tiny room at night. During the day I did jobs for them, cooking and cleaning and washing, trying not to make them angry because I didn't know what would happen if I did . . .' She pauses, taking a deep breath. 'My uncle had to work at the nearby farm. I saw him at the weekend . . . The first few times we met, he cried. I'd never seen him cry.' She glances at DC Winter. 'I know you think my uncle is mean or stupid, but he was always trying to think up ways that we could escape. But we were scared.' She swallows. 'You see, they beat him, told him that he owed them money for our transport to this country and that he would have to work for six months to pay off their debt before he even started to earn any money.'

She stops again. I squeeze her hand. 'You can do it, Caterina,' I say quietly, although I don't know if I would want to tell people these things in a room with a recorder and no window.

'They watched television all the time, eating crisps and pizzas while I went backwards and forwards with more food. And more drink. I had to serve them like I was a maid and then clean up the mess around them and then go and wash up or make their beds – that was a horrible job. I could smell the sheets. Their sweat. Sometimes they were drunk, and that was scary. One time, the man, he was called Andrei, threw a bottle at me because I didn't bring a new one quick enough . . . But when they were just a *little* drunk, it was better, because they would forget about me and leave me alone.

'My uncle heard one of his work colleagues saying that I was getting older, looking like a teenager, and pretty or something like that.' She winces. 'My uncle was terrified that I might be sent away to somewhere even worse. So, he came up with a plan . . .

'My uncle told me that on Fridays there was usually a different person in charge at the farm and most times after work they'd visit someone on the way back to where they slept . . . It had something to do with money . . . The workers would usually be left outside in the truck for ten minutes while he went into this man's house. My uncle thought that if he had a few minutes head start he could probably get to the woods which were only a few minutes away and then he could escape . . .'

'That was the plan?'

Caterina's eyes dart all over the place, looking around the room and at the door until they stop for a moment, as if she's seeing something in the corner, although I can't see anything. She swallows.

'Do you want more water?' DC Winter asks, handing over a large jug.

'Yes, please,' she says.

'Or something else? Juice? Tea or coffee?'

'No, this is fine,' she says, sipping the water.

'So, what happened Caterina?' DC Winter asks. 'Can you go on with the story?'

'Yes,' she mutters, although her lips are quivering. 'That was the plan. But we had to leave at the same time, and it was difficult for me because, at night, they locked me in a room, and during the day they were just there, mean and drunk and scary . . .' Caterina takes a deep breath. 'Anyway, I pretended to have stomach aches for two days, from the Wednesday until the Friday of the week of the escape, gradually increasing them, pretending to double over in pain, going to the bathroom for longer and longer periods so that they wouldn't be suspicious. I realised that the glass in the bathroom window was thin. I thought I could probably break it as there was a small crack running through it already, but the window was so small that I'd have to remove all the glass before I could get through.

The last time I went in, when they were almost asleep, I took a towel. I wrapped it around my hands and pushed it through the window as quietly as I could. I'd laid another towel down on the floor so that the glass wouldn't shatter and fall on the tiles. I knew the sound would be loud, but I had to keep pushing against the glass until enough had broken away from the frame. And then I managed to crawl my way through the window. I only cut my arm here.' She points to a thin, mauve line on her left arm. 'Then I ran towards the trees.' She stops, scrunching up her face but then looks down, twisting the fingers on her left hand. 'I had been there ninety-four days when I escaped.'

'What was the plan once you reached the trees?' DC Winter asks.

'My uncle told me to walk two kilometres north and then a kilometre east and then to wait. He would make the sound of a particular bird, like an owl, that used to live near our house and so I would know it was him. And that it was safe.'

'How did you know how far a kilometre was?'

'Well, I had a rough idea, but I also counted my steps.' Caterina rubs her eyes.

'You're doing really well, Caterina,' DC Winter says.

'It was a cloudless nights with a full moon and I sat for hours, listening for sounds, and I was terrified. I stared up at the moon and I tried to focus on it. Something bright. And, you know, constant.' She bites her lip and looks at me. 'I told myself that, as long as I kept looking at it, I would be somehow protected – that there were bigger, more powerful things than that horrible Kristof gang . . . like the sun and moon and stars . . . things that were more remarkable.' A tear starts falling down her left cheek, which she roughly brushes away. 'And, eventually, my uncle came. Eight long, horrible hours later, he found me . . .'

'I know this might sound like a silly question, but why didn't you think to go to the police once you managed to get out?' asks DC Winter gently.

'Those people said we owed them money,' Caterina says simply. 'And, you know, the police in our hometown weren't all good people. Some of them just turned away when bad things happened.' But she looks around, her eyes wide. She suddenly doesn't seem sassy or confident or wise at all, but like a child. A terrified child. I move closer to her, covering her hands with mine. I can feel her hands trembling and quivering. And something makes me think of the bird, scared and alone and defenceless, hovering in my hands until someone can find its home.

It's late when Dad knocks on my door. 'Are you alright?' he asks. I nod, although I can't speak. 'Grandma messaged me to say that the Boston museum sent another batch of letters.' He comes into the room and hands me the package. 'She sent you another parcel.' He has a small frown on his face. 'Perhaps tomorrow though?'

'OK,' I say. 'From Mary or Ruby?'

'Both,' he says. 'So maybe we will find out what happened after the boat. And if Mary actually got away permanently . . .'

He comes over and hugs me. I can smell soap and a faint smell of sweat, but I don't mind it. 'Do you think Caterina will be OK now?' I ask.

'I hope so,' Dad says. 'It must have been horrendous for her . . .but sometimes releasing all of that hurt and pain can help you to start moving forwards.'

'I know,' I pull back a little, still holding one of Dad's

hands although I can't quite look straight into his eyes. 'I think she's helped me to understand that too . . .You know, Caterina had so many bad things happen, but she still keeps going. She still survives.'

'Clover,' he says. 'I think you were a really good friend to her today.'

I lean into him, trying to stifle my sobs. Dad makes strange shushing noises, but he just stays there, letting me cry. I can't even explain why properly. But it was something about him saying I was a really good friend. He wouldn't know, not for sure, but I had never really had a friend before.

Chapter Thirty-Nine

Mary

November, 1851
Dear R,

My throat's like straw when I wake up. For a few seconds I don't know where I am and then I see Samson, standing by the door. 'Here,' he says, handing me a cup of water but, even after every last drop has gone down, my throat feels still feels dry, and I have to swallow to stop myself from being sick.

I try to get to my feet. Samson holds my hand to steady me, but the room still turns so much I have to focus on the floor.

'Mary, you gotta neaten down your clothes and hair,' he says, handing me a knee-length beige coat. He gives me a strange grin. 'One of our brothers works here. He didn't ask any questions, but he let me have this. It's colder here and it will cover up those clothes anyway.' I put on the coat, smoothing down my hair, but it's just a cloud of wisps and strands. 'You supposed to be my sister. You gotta look a little bit refined,' he says, smiling at his joke.

'We're here?' I ask. 'We're in the North?'

'Yep. Gotta take you to some folks over the other side of town, but it's crawling with patterollers since that Fugitive

Slave Bill, so we still need to walk off this boat like we own the world.'

I stagger a few steps, but my feet are numb after being wedged between a chair leg and box but, when Samson opens the door, a gust of cool air hits my face and, as soon as I take a few breaths, the tightness in my chest disappears. We walk along a corridor until we reach the narrow staircase. Samson creeps to the top step, beckoning me to follow but my legs are still not moving right, and I stumble up the steps.

'Shush,' he says, anxiously looking around. 'Gotta get up one more level at least before we can be seen.' The blood slowly works its way through to my feet as we climb the next set of stairs and reach a door. 'Now, take my arm,' Samson says. I hold on to his elbow, feeling the tightness of his muscles, forcing myself to look ahead until we reach the gangway.

Most people have already left the boat. A few women, dressed in silk and satin with layers of frills that remind me of Ruby's dolls, are leaning over the sides of the boat, waving fans. A woman with hair the colour of flames and a thick layer of white make-up on her face looks me up and down, noticing the creases in my dress peeping out under the coat. Samson tips his hat. 'Hello again,' he says, all confidence and a big, wide smile.

I look out towards the dock. 'Boston,' Samson whispers with a little nod and smile of satisfaction. There's noise and music and colour – horses braying and carriage wheels turning, people calling to each other and the sounds of gulls overhead against the sharp music from organs and horns of boats. My heart starts to fly until I see two men, big hats and guns in their holsters, a few metres away from the gangway of the boat. One of the men spits high into the air – an arc that ends a few inches away from our feet. The other man fiddles with the handle of his gun, a horrible smirk on his face.

As we follow the line towards the gangway, my heart is racing. Just as we are going to get off the boat, the woman with hair like flames just in beside me. 'Want some company?' She asks Samson. For a second I don't know what she means but then she narrows her eyes. 'Might help,' she mutters with a small nod towards the men in the distance.

For a few seconds Samson doesn't say anything. He studies the woman's face. I think he is trying to work out whether to trust her. 'That will be mighty fine,' he says eventually in a voice that I haven't heard him use before.

The woman takes his arm. As we walk down the gangway, Samson forces a broad smile. I take a deep breath because I need to hold myself together. I can't be caught now. After coming all this way. The woman speaks loudly, keeping the conversation going about the weather and the fine theatres that Boston has. I walk as tall as I can past the men, holding my breath even though their eyes are balls of fire. One of them spits in the air again. It lands on my shoe. I feel sick but I ignore it, hearing the cackle of one of the men laughing.

When we get to the first street, the woman lets go of Samson's arm. She gives a little nod to him, and he tips his hat. 'Mighty obliged to you,' he says as she walks off down a side street. We don't say anything else, until we have walked at least a kilometre.

It's only then that Samson glances around. No one is behind us. He whistles softly and I feel like I can breathe again. 'Reckon those men are here about someone else,' he mutters. 'But definitely patterollers. I'd know those savages anywhere.' And then his voice becomes low and serious. 'Miss Mary. That is the last time anyone going to spit on you without you – or me or anyone else – saying anything.'

'I promise,' I say, looking straight ahead, and give him a little smile, which just about stills the tremor in my cheek.

Chapter Forty

Clover

The morning Ms Delauney leaves the hostel she asks me to go for a walk. She wants to say goodbye to the heath. 'So much colour,' she says with a little nod at the rows of yellow and purple flowers. 'It was just this blanket of green but look at it now.'

'My mum always noticed all the colours and . . .' My voice trails off.

Ms Delauney looks at me, her eyes narrowed. 'The detail?' I nod.

'Clover, *you* notice the detail in things too. It's why you've been so helpful with my research.'

I try not to blush, but I can't help smiling. 'What will you do next? Now your research is finished, I mean. Where will you go?'

'Well, an old colleague of mine has lined up a few lectures in London, although I'm afraid I'll be slightly rusty after all this isolation . . . and then perhaps I will start another project.' She glances at me. 'How are you feeling about moving?'

'I'm a bit scared about school. I mean, I didn't know

how to *be*, exactly. I mean, I know that sounds a bit weird. I could talk to Mum. We could talk for hours . . .but everything else seemed hard. But now, after all this – you know, Caterina, and you and Dad,' I say quietly. 'Well, I think, at least I can make friends now.'

'I'm sorry you were so lonely.'

'It wasn't all bad. I mean, Mum and me really did have lots of fun too . . . But it made making friends scary, because I thought I'd never fit in.'

'So, what changed?'

'I suppose I realised that I don't have to be like that. I mean, lots of people *aren't* the way I thought you had to be. All cool clothes and confident. Caterina isn't like that. And Heather isn't either. I mean, Heather was really cool in a different way. She didn't care about impressing everyone or being anything except what she was.'

For a few seconds she just carries on walking a few paces away from me, although I can tell she's thinking about something. 'Clover,' she says eventually. 'Did I ever tell you about Anancy?'

'I don't think so,' I say. But then I remember. 'Maybe you did once, but I didn't really know who he was.'

'Well, he's a character from Caribbean folk stories. He first came from Africa, travelling across the waters within the memories of all those who were stolen from their homeland into slavery. And, at night, after labouring all day in the horrendous conditions of the plantations, Anancy and the stories offered some kind of way of fighting back . . . They reminded people of where they came from and that, even though Anancy was physically weak, he would find a way to survive and, sometimes, even win.'

I thought about something Mary said. 'Was he like Brer Rabbit?'

'Yes, I suppose he was in many ways. They both offered a sort of secret language so that the people on the plantations could tell stories at night and no one could properly understand all their hidden meanings but them.' She glances at me. 'But I only understood recently what those stories must have meant to my mum . . . I think they gave her a sense of rootedness and pride. And so, she knew that she could be different and that, even if people tried to shut her out, she felt like she could find some kind of place in the world.' She smiles, a small, straight flash. 'I think she was trying to fill me and my sister with that confidence. And only now can I see how hard it must have been for her, coming from the Caribbean to Britain in the 1940s, wanting to be something – a doctor, perhaps – and yet being turned away, humiliated.'

'Do you think that's why you love myths? Because of all those stories?'

'You asked me that before. On the heath that first day.'

'Did I?'

'Yes, I didn't really know the answer then. But you're right. Sometimes I imagine I'm telling my mum the stories and myths that I love so much and, it might sound strange, but I always try to listen to what she thinks.'

She looks at me and, for a second, I see her eyes fill with tears but then she gives me, a broad, warm smile and her eyes sparkle.

'Maybe that's something that you need to find, Clover. A way of keeping your mother alive. A way that she can talk to you.' She pauses. 'And you to her.'

Chapter Forty-One

Mary

November, 1851
Dear R,

This is how my story starts. Or ends. I can never work out which, so maybe it's a circle – never beginning or ending, just continuing through time.

Samson took me to live with a family called the Garretts. For the first time I can remember, I lie in a proper bathtub, warm and frothy as the soap forms a delicate layer of bubbles on the top of the dull water. I let my hair fan out behind me, floating as I stare at the ceiling. I wonder what Martha and Rachel are doing. Whether they are feeding the chickens or whether Tildy will be in the kitchen making cornbread. I hope she'll smile at the thought of me free, although I miss her big, warm hugs all the time.

The Finch cabin seems a long way away. Now I sleep in a bed with clean sheets that smell of blossom and, every night, the golden glow of the moon comes in through the window.

I think about Samson, wishing I'd said more than a muffled 'thank you' as he went away. I was trying not to cry because I knew I'd miss him, but I think he still understands how grateful I am.

I wish I could write a letter to Tildy and to Rachel and to Martha. To try to send over a little piece of this freedom, so they might sense it carried on the breeze, just as sometimes I heard my momma's voice, like a whisper in the night sky. And that one day they will also be able to take their own shoes off in a place where they are free, to walk around a garden and feel the soil and grass under their feet, the small worms and insects that might wriggle and crawl beneath them, tickling their toes.

I wish I could send Rachel the scent of the flowers and let her run her long fingers over the waxy petals so she can remember how colours feel, bold and bright and vivid, like a wonderful painting. A different type of world, so she won't have nightmares anymore.

And I think about Benjamin. And Ruby, reading on the wooden floor, which reminds me of the golden bark of a forest of trees, her delicate finger tracing the journey that the rivers run through, glimpsing clues about places she dreams of visiting.

But the sense of weightlessness and calm as my hands paddle in the water and my skin shines with a layer of moisture, smooth and clean, is still the best feeling in the world.

I dress slowly, pulling on the stiff dress in indigo blue and brushing my hair as many times as I can. I walk past hardback books on the shelves, and pictures on the wall in browns and greens, distant landscapes, framed in ornate, chunky frames which somehow clash with the plain walls. It's not as grand as the Finch house, which was all lace and china, but it's a house you can breathe in, with the sounds of violins and a smell of polish and bread.

My hand slides down the banister of the wide staircase until I reach the bottom step. Miss Garrett smiles at me, her eyes twinkling as we walk into the living room. 'Come and join us for some tea,' *she says.*

The table is laid with sparkling cutlery on a plain tablecloth, a jug of water and cups and candles in the centre, and I sit opposite Mr Garrett and between his two sisters, Faith and Margaret.

I eat silently, the delicious soup slipping down my throat, wanting to take as long as I can to enjoy the bursts of flavours.

And then Margaret Garrett smiles at me. 'When you are recovered and quite well, we could introduce you to some boys or girls of your age. And then perhaps you could start some lessons. I could teach you to read, if you like.'

I hesitate at first and then I say quietly, 'I would like to be able to read better.'

'You can read already?' *she asks, surprised.*

'A little,' *I say.*

And then I take a deep breath and add, 'You have been so kind to me, but I need to ask something even more of you.' *I look up at them.* 'I need to find my brother.'

Chapter Forty-One

Clover

They get to the hostel in the middle of the afternoon. Caterina is first out of the taxi. Her hair looks brushed and shiny, and she has an energy that wasn't there before. Like this is how she should have been, if she wasn't hungry and ill and struggling to survive in a hut on a heath.

'Come in,' Dad says, extending his arm. 'Shall we sit on the lawn? Enjoy the sunshine?'

Caterina's uncle smiles, although he looks weak still, despite his groomed appearance in a clean, pressed shirt and trousers. He sits down in the chair, after cautiously navigating his way around the table, although his hands don't seem to be shaking as much as they were before.

'Shall we go for a walk?' I say to Caterina. Her eyes dart over towards her uncle, but he smiles encouragingly at her, turning back to Dad, who's pouring coffee from a cafetière.

We walk to a cluster of trees at one side of the building, a collection of elms which shade the grass. 'Is that a new skirt?' I ask, suddenly not sure what to say and not wanting to ask about the enormous subjects yet – like the court case and moving away.

'Yes,' Caterina says. 'DC Winter – Lauren – brought it over.'

'Green suits you.'

She laughs. 'Well, it's not exactly what I would have chosen, but it's nice to have clean clothes – and it's nice to *be* clean.'

'Let's climb the tree,' I say, looking up at the branches full of leaves golden and glowing in the sun. Most days, now that it's warmer, I walk round the garden after tea and, if Dad isn't there, I climb up through the branches, the sun catching light on the leaves.

'OK!' Caterina says with a little look of surprise, but she grins and starts climbing. 'Do you think this is *cool* behaviour?' she asks, smiling. 'I mean, is this what teenagers do?'

'I wouldn't know ... I like it though,' I call out, following her, until we get to the top of the tree, and manage to find a branch horizontal enough to sit on.

'You're right,' Caterina says, looking around. 'It is beautiful here.' The sea glistens in the distance, and light catches on the waves – tiny luminous points on the water's surface.

'We'll probably leave soon,' I say, glancing at Caterina.

'Where will you go?'

'To Dorset. To a house near the sea.' I can't look at her. 'What do you think? I think maybe it could be good there.'

'Well, you like the sea.'

'What about you, though?' I ask. I can't shake the feeling that I'm abandoning her.

'It depends,' she says.

'What about your home?' I ask. 'Would you go back there?'

'There's nothing *there*,' she tries to say breezily, but her throat catches, and she puts her hair behind her ears, staring at me. 'Clover, did I ever tell you about my mother?'

'A little,' I say.

'Well, she had hair a bit like mine, except it was thicker and fell down her back in waves,' Caterina says eventually. 'You would have been able to draw a more beautiful picture of her than me.' She tries to smile but it seems trapped on her face. 'I don't really remember her that well. It was my uncle who made me a swing. It was on thick rope hanging down from a tree and the seat was a wooden circle. I loved that swing . . .' Her forehead furrows into deep creases and, in that moment, she seems much older than fourteen.

'Caterina,' I ask, 'would you like to have the picture I drew of you?'

'No,' she says, shaking her head. 'But thank you.' And then she adds, 'I mean, I really like it, but it's yours.'

'Well, I'll put it on my wall when we move to Dorset then,' I say. 'I'm not saying it's a work of genius or anything, but it will remind me of you.'

'Really?' she asks, her eyes shining. 'I must be important.'

'You *are*,' I say. 'And, I mean, we can call all the time anyway.' Caterina flashes a big, wide smile.

'This is really peaceful,' I say, looking around. 'This is somewhere I feel like I can just *be* . . . Do you know what I mean?' Caterina doesn't say anything. She just moves the hair that keeps flying into her eyes behind her ear. 'Ms Delauney always says that we're all just nomads moving around and finding a bit of earth to live on, and we can either add to it or take something away.'

'I like that,' Caterina says. 'I hope *I* add something one day . . .'

'Me too,' I say.

'Listen,' Caterina says. 'Listen to the air and the sea. That rhythm . . . the breeze swirling in and out and all around us. It's like we're all part of the same earth. And the same air.'

'Yes,' I say, thinking about Mary and Ruby and Benjamin. And how people can help and influence each other in a spider's web of layers and circles. I suddenly wonder if that's what Ms Delauney meant with her stories about Anancy the spider too. 'We're all connected somehow, don't you think?' I say. 'I mean, we can all be important to each other's lives. We have the power to make them worse.'

'Or better,' Caterina says, her eyes twinkling and her smile growing wider and brighter as she looks at me.

Chapter Forty-Three

Clover

'It still doesn't make sense,' I say, as Dad and I hover over a plate of warm croissants, gazing out of the window at the rain-drenched cobbled streets. We're on our way to Winchester again and are poring over sheets and sheets of writing at a little café. 'The dates of the letters, who Mary was writing to – *any* of it... We don't even know why Mum had that piece of quilt. I mean, I know it was sort of relevant but...'

'I agree. It doesn't add up.' Dad frowns. 'Do you think they caught Mary eventually? Do you think that the paddyrolls, or whatever they were called, came for her, and that they enforced that Fugitive Slave Law and took her back?'

'I don't think so,' I say. 'That would be terrible...' I look at him. 'I don't know if I want to know what happened if it turned out badly – if Mary has to change so that she doesn't go on telling her amazing stories and Benjamin isn't bothered by the evil of it all.'

'And Ruby?' he asks, flicking the flaky crumbs from his hands.

'I hope that she protests about things.'

'Me too,' Dad says. He glances at me with a little frown. 'It could turn out bad though, Clove.'

'I know,' I say.

When we're finished at the café, we go for a walk. There's a small parade of shops with a pharmacy and a jewellery shop with stands filled with hairbands.

'I'd like to buy something for Caterina,' I say going into the pharmacist.

Dad trails after me while I choose a fluorescent nail varnish, and hairbrush and comb set in a make-up bag, and a lip balm in the shape of a Siamese cat.

'Do you think that's it for her now?' I ask Dad, on our way back to the car, thinking about the court case that she might have to give evidence at. 'I mean, she won't have to dredge it all up – those horrible memories – all over again?'

'I hope not . . .' He frowns. 'But I fear that she might. Maybe even be asked to go into more detail.'

'Oh God,' I say, remembering Caterina's face in that interview. 'Do you have to be so honest *all* the time . . . ?'

'Well, I'm my daughter's father,' Dad says with a half-smile. 'Anyway, at least they've caught the gang, and they'll go to prison.'

'What do you mean?' I ask, stopping still for a moment.

'What, the honesty thing?' he asks. 'Or about the gang?'

'The honesty thing,' I say.

'I just meant that you always tell the truth.' He shrugs. 'At first, it could be kind of difficult to take, but then I realised that I wouldn't have it any other way, and so I sort of promised myself that I would do the same.'

We walk through a churchyard, along a narrow lane, past a patch of green lined with yellow and purple pansies. 'Dad, where's *your* family?' I ask. 'I mean, what happened to them?' His eyes dart over at me, scanning my face like he's trying to work out how to respond. 'You don't *have* to say . . .' I say quietly.

'No,' he says, his voice firm, although I see a flash of pain as he looks down at the border of flowers. 'My dad wasn't such a nice man,' he says, his lip quivering. 'Well, actually, he was worse than that. He was a vile, abusive husband to my mum.' He swallows. 'And a terrible father.'

'Oh.' I want to say that I'm sorry, but it seems too irrelevant somehow, so I put my arm through his, walking with him the way Caterina did once when we were coming back from the stream. Dad doesn't look at me, but he grips my hand.

'Dad,' I say, once we're almost back at the car. 'That thing you wrote the day you left . . .'

'Yes,' he says.

'I felt like there were bits missing.'

'Like what?'

'Well, I still don't get it.'

Dad looks at me. I can't explain, but it doesn't make sense. Everyone says that Dad's a good person. Grandma and Ms Delauney obviously like him. And I see it too now. Maybe I've always seen it, but tried to bury it because, if Dad was kind and principled, then maybe it was Mum who was in the wrong, which felt too difficult to cope with. But then I think about Ruby and her Mama and how they changed. So, maybe it wasn't simple. Maybe everything was more intricate and detailed. Like a spider's web. Or a patchwork quilt.

I take a deep breath and look right at him. 'It was Mum, wasn't it?' I ask quietly. 'She told you to leave, didn't she?' But it isn't really a question, and Dad doesn't nod or say yes. He just carries on looking ahead, a quick flash of tears in his eyes.

Chapter Forty-Four

Clover

It's late afternoon when we get back. The hostel feels strange and empty without Ms Delauney, and I realise that, apart from not seeing Caterina, I won't be sorry to leave the featureless dining room and the boxlike bedroom. I glance over at the window, expecting to see her sitting there, pen in hand and that small, curious smile and look of complete concentration on her face.

'Do you want to have tea now or later?' Dad asks.

'I'm going to wash my hair first,' I say.

There's a pile of post outside my room. A short postcard from Ms Delauney saying she's settled into her 'digs' and that she'll see us in three weeks 'once we're settled' at the new house. There's also a parcel and, when I open it, there's a note at the top from Priya.

> *The museum finally got hold of some letters from*
> *the Finch plantation in Georgia.*
> *Best wishes.*
> *P. x*

I glance at the first page, my eyes racing through the words.

'Dad,' I call, running down the stairs two at a time. He's in the dining room, a half-amused expression on his face as he watches me.

'Look!' I say, sitting down at the table and laying out the pages in front of us.

December 12th, 1851
Dear Ruby,

I send this message via my good friend who is shortly travelling to Georgia as I am loathe to trust this to the postal system and the risk of someone else reading this information.

Unexpectedly last week, Zane, a quite exceptional young man of colour, who works at the Boston Vigilance Committee brought me some news about a family called the Garretts who, he told me, had a young girl living with them. A sixteen-year-old girl called Mary.

Ruby, Mary visited me the next day, appearing in my front room at ten sharp – a poised, artistic girl with a sweet smile and fire in her eyes.

Of course, Mary's greatest concern is to find Reuben, her brother. She has been working with Zane to help those runaways who find themselves in the North. As you can imagine they are still vulnerable, and often without family or the means to make much money.

I could see why you were so taken with her. I sensed the purpose in her words, and the determination in her eyes. I can only hope that she and Zane are successful in tracing her brother who, someone has reported, is at a plantation near the River Ohio.

I don't know what it will mean to you, but as Mary left, she paused, a few words on her lips whilst she considered what to say, before she turned, and her eyes locked onto mine.

Ruby, she told me to tell you that she missed you and your evenings telling stories and imagining journeys through the rainforest.

Your loving aunt,
Iris

December 20th, 1851
Dear Aunt Iris,

I read your letter five times, and I confess that I thought my heart would leap right out of my chest.

Today I followed behind Papa as he walked around the plantation, visiting Abraham and Tildy and Martha and Rachel. He has finally done what Grandpa intended. He didn't say why exactly. I would have liked to think I played a part. Or Benjamin constantly nagging him. But in truth, I think it was lots of things. Because, since Mary left everything seems different. And since that awful day with Matthias, Mama has changed too. The legal papers have been drawn up. Papa has given everyone their freedom, although he has asked them to stay, to work for a small salary and a share of the profits. He promises that he will build bigger, better cabins and that each person will have a small allotment to grow vegetables and bonuses if the plantation can still make a decent profit.

Afterwards, Martha walked up to Papa, her head high and chin jutting out in the way she does and said, with her eyes ferocious, 'I wish I could leave. Maybe one day I will leave. One day when my momma can breathe better. But, for the moment, we accept your offer.'

Tildy cried with joy when I told her about Mary, but Martha gave a small, satisfied nod, tears in her eyes. 'She did what we all dreamed of,' I heard Martha say. 'She was always clever. Always seemed like someone who could make it.' And then she swallowed. *'Thought I might have done too, if I'd had the chance . . . How I would have loved to walk on the ground and feel the insects in the damp earth and feel totally free.'*

Aunt, I watched as Tildy hugged Martha.
I think it is the first time I ever heard Martha laugh.
Your loving niece,
Ruby

I look over at Dad as he reads the last page, seeing him clench his fist before he opens up his fingers again.

'That's incredible,' he says, looking at me with tears in his eyes.

'I know,' I say, but he still sees my frown.

'Then what is it?'

'I'm still worried about Mary,' I say. 'We don't know exactly what happened. Even with all those letters and the research, Grandma never quite worked out what happened to Mary and the business and everything.'

I almost expect Dad to say that it's absurd, that it's waited one hundred and seventy-five years so can probably wait a few more days. But he smiles.

'Then we'll find out,' he says.

Chapter Forty-Five

Clover

'Good to see you two again,' Priya says as she shows us to the conference room, placing a tray with a cafetière and jug of water on the table, before closing the door.

There's a low hum of air conditioning as I stare at the list of documents that Priya has found for us. She told us not to be hopeful – she thought there wasn't anything else left and, at first, it does just look like monotonous details about contracts and notes about board meetings and transactions, which seem unbelievably dull.

Dad studies the first page, running his finger down beside the names and the dates. 'The obituary said that Benjamin came to this country in 1858. He would have been about twenty-four or twenty-five, but I can't see that the money he used came with him from the plantation in Georgia. Apart from the loan from Nicholas Stemming-Stokes, all those documents that show that he did apprenticeships, and the newspaper articles as well suggest that he earned it himself.'

Dad keeps scanning the pages and I keep searching, working my way through the other lists of documents that Priya found.

At some point I notice Dad's pen hovering above another entry, out of the corner of my eye. 'What is it?' I ask.

'I'm confused about what happened to Mary – I'm wondering whether she went back to the plantation,' he says quietly. 'Otherwise, I don't understand how they still have her letters.'

'No,' I say, a bit too loudly. 'That doesn't make sense. She was working with that man Zane to help runaways. '

'I don't get it either. I thought maybe R was Reuben, but I don't know if he was ever rescued . . . unless Mary just imagined that she was telling him her story.' I think about how often I want to tell Mum about something that happened to me, especially after what Ms Delauney said about how I should find a way to keep her alive.

'I think we should go,' Dad says. 'We've been here hours. Maybe we won't ever know . . . I mean, so many documents were destroyed in the fire.'

I have a sinking feeling in my chest and glance up at the clock, its loud ticking suddenly irritating. Because I want to know that Mary had a good ending. That she had a happy life after such a horrible start. And Ruby and Benjamin too. I need to know that Ruby stayed strong. That she didn't eventually get changed by the world.

'Just a bit longer,' I say, racing through the stack of pages in front of me, although most are boring lists of minutes and transactions. I scan all the details, my eyes sore from the effort of studying shapes and dots and numbers or letters.

'OK,' Dad says, looking back down at his pile.

I go through each page in front of me again. There's still a lot of initials being thrown around – the BF and MCS I noticed before. But in these pages, it's clear MCS makes a lot of the decisions. It's MCS who puts forward an idea for a scholarship fund for underprivileged children and who suggests appointing more women to good positions and is determined to ensure decent conditions for the staff.

'Dad, who's MCS? I mean, aren't we ignoring something here? The company isn't just about what Benjamin does. There are other people that do a lot too.'

'Good point.'

But then I notice something, my eyes hovering above a particular entry. 'Dad.'

'What is it?'

'There's an entry which doesn't seem to relate to anything else. It says: *Letter addressed to RF, dated May 1861.* It could be Ruby Finch, couldn't it?'

Dad stands behind me, his hand lightly touching my arm. 'And look,' I say, my voice trembling. '*Look* who it says it was written by.'

'MCS,' breathes Dad.

Maybe it was because the name didn't mean anything then and so I'd only looked through the documents for the name *Benjamin, or BF*. But now, it comes crashing down, a whirl of ideas that are suddenly clear. And *obvious*. And within that haze appears the memory of a child who kept me company at the house in Scotland at night sometimes, more real than anyone believed.

'Come on,' I say, gently tugging Dad out of the room until I break into a run, going towards the family tree in its thick ornate frame. 'I didn't understand when I looked before. It's a common enough name. And the other names didn't mean anything.'

I glance at Dad, placing my finger over my name at the bottom and then move it, following the meandering thread through Mum and Grandma and then further back in little ink tributaries, towards Ruby, until it settles on Benjamin.

And next to him is MCS.

Mary Cecilia Samson.

'Dad,' I call out, my voice somewhere between a laugh and tears. 'We didn't realise before.'

'What do you mean?' Dad asks.

'She must have changed her name to Samson . . . but this has to be Mary. *Our* Mary.'

Chapter Forty-Six

Mary

May, 1861
Dear R,

You may think this isn't part of my story at all, and yet it is. Because the stories are part of our lives, and we have to find some place within the world. Not just my story inside that gives me that place to go to, like a little piece of the sky and the moon and stars, but a small corner where we can be the centre.

You asked me once to tell you about the stories as if it was as easy as telling you the name of a tree, but I couldn't explain why it wasn't like that at all and ended up shaking my head and just saying that they were 'special'. Because, on the plantation, when the stars sprinkled across the indigo sky, stories were a remarkable, magical secret, a thread that meandered in and out of different lives, creating a sparkling, protective web all around me. It wasn't even just my imagination that was in flight as it swooped between the stars and glowing moon. They gave us a little piece of humanity, reminding us of who we were, and where we came from. It was the same for every one of us. Brer Rabbit wasn't only a funny character so vain he dressed up in his waistcoats thinking that he was the single most important person there. He came to America on those terrible boats with our ancestors. He kept a little piece of Africa for us, and it helped me to stand firm and still, like I had the roots of a tree, connecting me to the ground and sky and to everything.

So, R, this is my story. Those pieces of me that could still find a place to breathe and exist when I was not ready to collapse in a kitchen so hot it felt like a piece of hell. It was the stories we told each other, Abraham's fiddle soaring like a bird, or the tapping rhythm of Martha's foot. And now I'm telling it to you, Ruby. Because I trust you.

Chapter Forty-Seven

Clover

It's eleven o'clock when Dad loads the last case in the boot. I turn to look at the hostel. It's just a tumbling down building but, even though I didn't think it would, it feels hard to leave the place. There were so many good things here. Memories of Ms Delauney and Caterina. And it was where I really got to know Dad. But I'm excited too, because I know I will make other memories. And probably friends. And the new house is not far from Grandma and my cousins and uncle and can be a proper home, near the sea.

'See you soon, Clo,' Caterina says, hugging me. 'Thank you.'

'For what?' I ask.

'You're a really good friend,' she says. 'I mean, you don't have to be cool or anything.'

I laugh. 'What do you mean?'

'You don't give up on people. I mean, not ever. And that's kind of cooler than however it is we're supposed to be.'

I try not to blush, tears filling my eyes, which I blink

away. 'I'll miss you,' I say, and she beams.

I don't open the parcel Ms Delauney's sent until we've driven for over half an hour. I just gaze out of the window, focusing on the drizzle and rain as the tears fall down my cheeks. Dad touches my hand once or twice, but he keeps his eyes on the road.

When I eventually peel back the layers of thin purple tissue, secured with tiny, fiddly patches of tape, I find a small book: *Cornwall's Knockers and Spriggans*.

There's a message inside the cover too – sprawling handwriting in blue ink.

> *To dear Clover,*
> *This was one of my first pieces of writing about Cornwall a few years ago – my first foray into the world of spriggans and knockers.*
> *When I met you, I rather imagined that you were a little like a stolen child. But, when you reach my age, you realise that everyone has strands, or threads, rather like that exquisite piece of fabric you shared with me, and that people will always see different things, like a bird, or simply triangles, but it doesn't mean that it's any less beautiful, or that the intention was any less beautiful.*
> *I will always remember our lovely spring together – how proud I am that you have learned the potential of your power, which we all have in one form or another.*
> *Your friend,*
> *Valerie Delauney*

I read it three times, remembering that first day, tramping across fields. Our feet stuck to the clumps of earth, and small white flowers forced their way out onto the heath. And Ms Delauney was energetic and enthusiastic, as if we were on a great adventure.

It starts as a small prickle, little sensations across my arms and chest. 'I think she's trying to tell me something about Mum,' I say, not realising I have said it out loud.

'What?' asks Dad.

'I think Ms Delauney is trying to tell me that Mum just made mistakes.' Dad's eyes stay fixed on the road. 'I get that she wasn't perfect. And I know that she loved me . . .'

Dad glances at me, a little frown across his forehead. 'What is it, then?'

'I just don't think I know how to remember her anymore.'

'Clover, we're all just muddling along, trying to get things right.'

'But *you're* not,' I say. 'You always do the decent thing . . .'

'Is that what you think?' he asks, his voice suddenly strained. 'Even after . . .' He doesn't finish his sentence, staying silent as he stares at the road until he gives a little cough, and I see him taking a deep breath. 'Maybe we've just got to find some way to cling on to her *essence*, Clover – her voice, her smile . . .'

'She loved colours,' I say, not knowing why. 'Purples and reds and indigo – all the dramatic ones. And she loved touching things. Sometimes it was a bit embarrassing,' I laugh, surprised at the bubbling sensation in my throat. 'If we were in a shop or a restaurant, she'd touch *everything*. The seats or the curtains, even.'

'I remember that about her,' Dad says, laughing.

'Dad, remember that day?'

'Which one?'

'The day you came to take me away.'

He nods but keeps looking straight ahead.

'I thought that I didn't want to say goodbye to the house, but I think maybe I was being stubborn or something and because you told me to do it . . .' My voice trails off.

'It's OK,' he says, and I let the softness of his voice settle the flurry in my chest.

'But, when we were driving through the gate, I looked back. I wanted to see the bit of garden she called "the wilderness", because she always said fairies lived there and I really believed her.' The memory suddenly seems so real it makes me jolt, the warmth of the sun on my face as we sat on the fraying blue and red picnic rug, each miniature bowl laden with ripe red strawberries, cut into quarters so that there's a sweet, juicy scent. *Summertime*. The best times. With the blackberries we collected from the hedgerows, glistening with sugar alongside minuscule plates with tiny morsels of fresh bread, still warm and dotted with already melting butter.

And *Mum*. Glowing and her hands moving around wildly, so that I watched them, opening and closing, one finger at a time, like a ballerina, chattering to invisible fairies.

'Mum could make everything seem magical.'

'I know,' Dad says. 'She did for me too. She was really special but, you know, you do that too.'

I look at him. 'Really?' I ask, wondering what he means. 'Do you mean that we just have to look for it? That it's how we see things.'

'Yes,' he says with a small smile.

It's late afternoon when we walk through the grey-blue gate of the small cottage, whitewashed with azure shutters at the windows, and long, lush fern green grass all around it. 'The sea's a few minutes' walk that way,' Dad says at the front door, the tiny patch of grass scruffy and overlong but still with that smell of moisture and dotted with daisies and buttercups in white and yellow.

There are three bedrooms, one small with a desk – Dad's new office – and a massive living room with a big window at the front. The walls are beige except for one wall in magenta.

'What do you think of the house, now that we're actually here?' Dad asks eventually. 'Not just looking at photos on a computer . . . Do you still like it?'

'I love it,' I say.

'The owner originally wanted to sell it but decided to rent it out instead. If we like it, though, she says we can buy it – update it a bit, you know, deck over the patio and get rid of some of this beige and grey.'

'That's good,' I say, staring out of the window towards the sea.

'How does it look?' he asks, smiling. 'Is it more blue or less blue than the sea in Cornwall?'

I glance at him. 'The sea's the sea. It's changing. All the time. It's a different mix of greens and blues and grey. Even a little dash of yellow.' He gazes out towards the bands of water in the distance, studying it for a few seconds until he gives a little nod of his head.

We walk around the house twice, silently opening cupboards and doors before going to the back garden, following the small path that divided the grass in two to the end. 'What's the little garden room out here for?' I ask, nodding towards it. 'I thought the study upstairs was for your work.'

'I thought you might like it as *your* space.' He glances

at me. 'Maybe for painting? Or you could learn an instrument? I used to play the guitar and piano. We could get a keyboard . . .'

'Really?' I ask, thinking again that there are a lot of things I still don't know about him. 'Is that what the psychologist suggested?'

'Maybe,' he says, with a little awkward grin, 'but I think it's a good idea anyway.'

Later, we walk down to the seafront. Dad keeps glancing at me. I can tell he's trying to work out how to say something.

'Clover . . .' he says eventually. 'I've thought about this so much that sometimes I think my mind is going to explode . . .' His voice trembles. 'I'm never going to get back all those years I lost with you and I'm always going to regret that.'

'It's OK,' I say, looking at him as I stand there, feeling the breeze in my hair and face.

'Whatever you feel is fine, but never ever question whether she loved you. She did. More than anything else in the whole world.'

Dad picks up a stone – a perfect smooth oval, flat and grey-blue. He throws it, skimming it across the surface of the water. 'I'll teach you,' he says as he makes it fly. I watch the stone, staring towards the sea, but Dad looks at me and smiles, and I sense a surge of something flow through me, almost like a gentle wave until it reaches my face and eyes and forces me to smile back.

It's early evening when we return to the house.

'I'm making a cup of tea. Do you want one, Clover?' Dad calls from the kitchen, but I'm wading through the bags and boxes, neatly piled up and labelled with a marker pen.

There's a collection of post, placed beside the door – random letters from the gas and electricity people – all the places that Dad meticulously contacted once he knew we were going to move. I flick through the variously sized envelopes until I find a card and a thick package in brown paper. The card is from Caterina and her uncle. She must have sent it a few days ago. *Happy happy new home!* is written in large, swirly writing. And then a few lines on the left side. *Write to me soon, Clover. Or better still call. I am getting a phone on Saturday so I can finally be a cool teenager . . .*

'Who's that from?' asks Dad as I carefully balance the card on the mantelpiece.

'Caterina,' I say.

'Do you know when she's starting school?' he asks.

'Next week. She seems excited . . . and her uncle likes his carpentry job.'

'Good,' Dad says, although the way he says it makes me wonder whether he knows more than he lets on, and whether some of those conversations and phone calls had something to do with the fact that Caterina's uncle now has somewhere to live and a job.

The other envelope is from Grandma. It's bulky with a wad of papers inside.

> *I hope the enclosed might help to explain the end of the story. They are probably the last of the documents that we will receive from the museum in Boston, discovered in an old box, which had been labelled incorrectly. It seems that the museum is now developing into quite a wonderful space. The curator is determined to share all these stories, including the marvellous work of*

the Boston Vigilance Committee, who helped so many people. For us too, I think these represent the last pieces of a metaphorical patchwork quilt.

I am so excited to visit you in your new home on Saturday. And I can't wait to hear your thoughts on so many things that we're working on here. You know, of course, that we have already started developing our own exhibition dedicated to Mary. It seems right to finally show all the work she did both in building the business and her insistence on decent working conditions and fairness. It is long overdue, of course. The company would not exist without her, so at least a few people will now know her name and something of her influence.

But I would also love your thoughts on something else – a scholarship fund that we're in the process of setting up. I am determined to try to repay at least some of the money that came from the profits of slavery in the Caribbean, and we have a number of other initiatives that we are working on. It cannot solve everything but, as far as we can, I would like to try to do a little good and hoped you might have an idea for a name?

'Did you say that you wanted tea?' calls Dad from the kitchen.

'Yes, please,' I say.

'What do you want to do for dinner? Get something from the village? Or make do with sandwiches tonight?'

I go into the kitchen. 'Dad, look,' I say, holding out the letter, my hands trembling with excitement. 'I know what the letters were about now. Mary was telling her story to

Ruby for the museum . . . Dad, Ruby must have gone and lived in Boston with Iris.'

'That's wonderful,' Dad says quietly.

'So, can we just sit and read these?' I ask.

Dad carries the drinks out to the patio. He gives a flash of a smile. 'Of course.'

'Grandma is asking me about another scholarship they are setting up. I wanted to suggest that it was named after Martha,' I say, thinking of how much Tildy wanted Martha to go to school.

Dad looks at me, his eyes flickering for a second. 'Yes,' he says. 'That's perfect.'

I place the pages of the letters on the table, but the sun goes behind a cloud, and I shiver. 'I'll get my jacket first, actually,' I say, jumping up. 'I don't want to be distracted when we find out the end of the story.'

I grab my coat from the hallway but, as I'm walking towards the back door, something catches my eye in the front room.

I stop, frozen for a few seconds. It's the painting. Dad must have put it up when I was looking through the post. Mum's last painting, above the fireplace, the light from the window illuminating the vivid colours of the trees and flowers. I move closer to the picture, studying every detail, trying to imprint every colour in my mind. And then I notice the birds, two swallows with their unmistakable silhouettes gliding above the hills.

'Look, Dad,' I say, hearing him walk back into the house to find me. 'I didn't notice them before . . . Grandma said that Mum wouldn't paint swallows, that she thought they were a cliché or something . . . but Mum painted this picture just before she became ill. She was up all night.' I wince, remembering that look of exhaustion all mixed in with pride as Mum showed me the picture. 'It was her favourite.'

Maybe Mum *knew* she was dying. Maybe there was some reason for that urgency.

'I think Mum was trying to tell Grandma that she was sorry,' I say, sensing a sudden lightness in my chest, everything coming together, all the patterns and strange irregular pieces finally slotting into place. Dad stands beside me, staring at the picture.

'When Mum died, I tried to imagine that this was the sort of place she'd like to be.'

'Her kind of heaven,' Dad says.

'Yes,' I say, glancing at him in surprise, thinking again of the kind of magic that Mum created, those moments of energy and excitement, and that love that she spun in a golden web, wrapping around me, illuminating everything.

Dad's standing so close I can feel his hand brush mine and hear his breathing. I don't know why but I take hold of his hand and feel him grip it back. I suddenly remember that feeling from when I was five or six and was scared. His massive hand and fingers bent around mine.

'I really loved her,' I say, a choke in my throat that I can't shake.

As we stare at the colours of the painting, my shoulder touches his arm and, for a few seconds, it feels like I could be floating as well, surrounded by that air and light.

'Me too,' he says. Dad smiles and his blue-green eyes, which remind me of the sea, gently twinkle.

We stay there for a few moments, breathing in the colour, until I say, 'Come on.' We walk back outside to the table where, sitting so close that our arms and feet touch, we begin to read.

Chapter Forty-Eight

Mary

Highgate, London, October, 1861
Dearest Ruby,

I can finally finish the story that you and Iris wanted for your museum. It's the last part that I haven't fully told you yet. The piece that doesn't only exist inside stories in my head that have been passed down through generations. You asked me to be unflinching when I told my story. To tell it from my perspective, as I lived it, and not to hold back. Sometimes that has been difficult. But I think we have a strong enough bond to get past those early moments when I thought you looked like a doll and didn't understand that your heart beat as strongly as I know it does now.

All I can say, Ruby, is that I know you. And you know me. And so I will imagine that we are next to each other in your room, lying on our fronts as we pore over books, the scent of blossom carried in on the breeze.

Benjamin thinks it all started with my momma. You see, I'd told him about her stories, and those dreams that made me feel that I could soar as high as a bird, trying to prise apart the terrible things that I felt and saw, sometimes almost every day, from that part inside that still felt like me. But it wasn't just Momma, but also Tildy and Martha, keeping on at me, to keep dreaming, to think that there might be something better, or somewhere better.

It was also you, though, Ruby ... Those moments when we would lie on the floor imagining distant places and adventures. It was you who wanted to climb mountains and see cities and rivers and the sea. So, I think that everything is related to everything else somehow. Like the interlinked birds and patterns of the quilts – those symbols that meant something. The signs that I learned, so that I could read the coded messages contained in the quilts to help us to find our way to freedom.

The day when Zane walked with me to your aunt Iris's door was one of those little links of the chain. I would have known that you were related anywhere, the way she held her head up, back tall and straight with eyes determined and ferocious. 'We couldn't find you,' she said.

'I changed my name,' I told her. 'Samson brought me here. He risked his life to help me reach freedom, so it seemed like a better name than the one forced on me because I was enslaved on a plantation.'

Faith and Margaret Garrett were kind to me from the first. Faith in particular was determined that I would go to university one day. She always was the hopeful one, believing that things could be wonderful, always picking out the red leaves in the tapestry of colour of fallen leaves around us. And one day, when we were out walking, a group of men and women emerged from the side of a small office building, I saw a man who looked like Reuben might look one day. He was wearing a suit and waistcoat and one of those hard hats that educated people and business people wear.

'This is Zane,' Faith Garrett said introducing us. 'He

works for the Boston Vigilance Committee.'

For a moment, I stared at him, wondering how Pete might have been if he could have lived a different life and if he could have turned his stories into writing that everyone would recognise, even though they were sometimes better than that – like an incredible theatre of sound and pictures.

'I would like to help,' I said to him. 'I know I'm young, but I can read and write a little.'

Zane smiled and it was such a wide, warm smile that I felt hope. 'Your age won't stop you,' he said. 'I am well acquainted with Miss Sarah Parker Remond, another of our fine women of colour, who was born right here in Massachusetts. She gave her first anti-slavery speech at your age.' And then he said something that made my heart give a leap. 'And I can tell that you also have a voice.'

You know the next part. Well, the practicalities of it, at least. That one day, when I was studying, I heard the ringing of the bell and walked to the door. And there was Zane, next to your aunt Iris, standing shoulder to shoulder as if forming a wall. And when they moved apart, just a few inches at first, I could see enormous brown eyes behind them. I think I wailed to the skies and stars as Reuben burst through and hugged me so tight that I thought he would never let me go, gripping my fingers so hard that his nails imprinted small horseshoes on my palm, minuscule marks that I wanted to keep forever.

It still feels strange to be here, in England, with the cool air. It's so green sometimes that it reminds me of the ocean – a blanket of colour that's somehow soothing. The pink and white blossom on the trees in spring and the willow trees dipping into the streams sometimes seem familiar. But there are lots of people from all parts of the world and different backgrounds here. There are literally thousands of people of colour in London. People from Asia and Africa and America as well as so many different parts of Europe. I suppose it is not surprising. England has for such a long time been a land of people flowing in and out, shaping it in their different ways. Recently, I saw a portrait of Olaudah Equiano that gave me courage. And so, when I first gave a speech to a room full of all kinds of people – elegant people in fine clothes and men and women of the working classes who labour in terrible conditions in factories, I thought I could see in their eyes that, even though many go home to their own families, they understood that we share a little of the same experiences. In England they hide their own history of slavery, but, for that moment, when they look me in the eye, and listen to my story, I realise that my voice has power. And that I can use it now. To speak loud and clear, reminding people how terrible and evil a thing slavery is, and that it still exists across the ocean. When I look at them, I hope that some of my words will have captured their imaginations and that they might remember Rachel and Tildy and Martha and my momma.

I can still smell the beautiful flowers of Georgia, and I still think of Tildy and Martha and Rachel. Some days I wish I could be with them, to feel part of that family, people who walked on the same scraps of earth as me and whose hearts remember the same heavy chains, but who also know the songs and the stories. I hope they speak a little more loudly or more irreverently now that they are free, and that they sing their hearts out to the soaring sound of the fiddle at night without fearing what might happen.

And, Ruby, I think of you too even though I am a whole ocean away from you – as the sun comes up and again when the sun sets, and when I look at Reuben carrying his hopes of going to university and becoming a zoologist.

You asked once why it was so easy to say yes to Benjamin when he came to Boston, standing at the doorstep, his hair falling over his eye before he told me of his plans. You are right. It was not exactly my dream to come to England, but I was given the opportunity, to study and to use my voice. And I thought of Samson's daughter and how he wanted her to have an education, and Sarah Parker Remond, who had the strength and courage to change things by studying at the University of London, and overcoming every obstacle to carve out her own unique path – and of all those other remarkable African Americans who came here before me, who tried to tell their stories, and make people listen. And so, I said yes. And later, when I'd studied and acquired a share of the business and a way of making money, I said yes to a different question of his.

Once or twice a week I still pull down the atlas you sent, tracing rivers and roads and imagining you and me sailing or floating along on the wave of our hopes.

I look at my mother's letter often too, her last words to me before she died. I imagine the birds that carried her to freedom, from safehouse to safehouse, and am thankful that we literally walked the same path and that she set her feet down on cool green grass and felt free.

I still sense her soul, flying high with the birds. And sometimes I dream so vividly of her that I wonder if she is there, beside me, or whether there is a part of my soul that is all mixed up with hers.

Your friend,
And sister,
Mary

Epilogue

November 9th, 1854
My dearest children, Mary and Reuben,

Iris Finch is writing this letter for me because, as you know, I cannot read and write. How useful that would be now.

But I believe that we are intertwined still, and that my heart hears yours, wherever we are.

I did not realise it at the time, but I followed in your footsteps, Mary, not sure how dangerous the journey might be.

I went to a safehouse just beyond Savannah. The lady at the house was tall and elegant and there was a storm that night. The trees battered on the windows and the leaves shook like God's hand was tapping on the glass, but we spent a night huddling together – she, terrified at the crashing of the thunder and the lightning – two women within a boarded-up old house.

To make the time pass, we started to sew, putting together pieces to make a new quilt. And that's when I looked again at the square with the flying geese.

I am not sure why, but I remembered the old sycamore maple tree, so I told her how I would tell stories to you under its shade.

And she remembered you, Mary. A sweet girl of sixteen

who thought those lines were birds and like little twirling sycamore leaves. And that you had headed north. Not defeated. Still my girl with a large heart and even finer mind. Still refusing to be beaten down.

She gave me the piece of quilt, a small fragment of fabric that I sewed into my clothes.

And it kept me alive. Kept me walking all those steps towards the North, knowing that you had travelled that path, praying that somehow you would be able to eventually carry Reuben there too.

It kept my heart swelling and singing on out as I walked barefoot on the earth.

Free.
Always free.
Your momma,
Cecilia

Acknowledgements

I started this story many years ago after visiting a tiny museum on an island in South Carolina in the USA. One of the exhibits was a quilt. Its individual squares represented a system of codes used to give information to enslaved runaways who were trying to escape to freedom. The image of the quilt stayed with me.

Much later, when I was studying for my MA, I focused my dissertation on the Brer Rabbit stories. These tales, adapted from their African origins, offered a vital form of communication for those enslaved on the plantations. It provided the foundation for a rich language and culture in the USA. It was at around this time that I started *Searching for the Remarkable in Things*, captivated by how the pieces of the quilt not only represented a path towards freedom but a wider message about the many strands of people's lives. I was also intrigued by the stories on the plantations and how they could create pockets of escape in people's minds. It was an idea that I further pursued in my PhD, looking at how a different set of stories, this time, tales of the entertaining, complex Anancy, offered ways to resist the brutal realities of the plantations in the Caribbean, informing ideas of identity and heritage.

At heart, *Searching for the Remarkable in Things* is a simple story about a teenage girl, Clover, trying to develop a sense of her identity. The backdrop to her journey are the lies she was told growing up about her family and origins. Ultimately, Clover's journey requires an understanding, not only of her family, but Britain's complex history encompassing its many waves of migration over hundreds of years. In this story Mary is enslaved on a plantation in the USA but, of course, until the 1830s many people were enslaved by the British in similarly horrific conditions in the Caribbean. When they were eventually freed, it was the enslavers who were paid massive sums of money in 'reparations' – money which then found its way into institutions in Britain.

It has taken a long time to get this story right. It has been guided throughout by my publisher, ZunTold, and especially Elaine Bousfield, who early on both saw and supported what I was trying to do. Thank you also to Isla Bousfield-Donohoe for understanding my vision and creating such a beautiful cover. Thank you also to ZunTold's copy editor, Melissa Hyder.

This book has also been inspired by my own personal experience and my research for my MA and PhD, paths that many people have contributed to. It has not always been an easy task to get everything right, and for the sections about Mary I am indebted to the encouragement and thorough eye of Kashinda Carter at the American-based Writing Diversely.

To my sisters – I hope that, when they read this story, they will recognise the small, distinct pieces that were influenced by our parents and will remember what they meant.

Finally, my thanks and love go to Jon, Amelie and Joe, who probably did not always understand what I was doing all this time but who were still enthusiastic and hopeful, which is everything after all.

For more insightful books you will love,
and to take part in our Living Books
and Storyteller community,
head to

zuntold.com